# THE HAUNTING

# THE HAUNTING

## Joan Lowery Nixon

DELACORTE PRESS

Published by
Delacorte Press
Bantam Doubleday Dell Publishing Group, Inc.
1540 Broadway
New York, New York 10036

**Library of Congress Cataloging-in-Publication Data**
Nixon, Joan Lowery.
    The haunting / Joan Lowery Nixon.
        p.      cm.
    Summary: When her mother inherits an old plantation
house in the Louisiana countryside, fifteen-year-old Lia seeks
to rid it of the evil spirit that haunts it.
        ISBN 0-385-32247-X
        [1. Ghosts—Fiction.  2. Haunted houses—Fiction.
3. Louisiana—Fiction.]  I. Title.
    PZ7.N65Hau   1998
    [Fic]—dc21                                    97-32658
                                                    CIP
                                                    AC

The text of this book is set in 12-point Goudy.

Manufactured in the United States of America

September 1998

10   9   8   7

BVG

For Allyson,
*who introduced me*
*to Louisiana's ghost*

# CHAPTER ONE

My fingers shook as I pushed back the long strands of hair that had fallen over my face. I peered at the pale, shriveled ninety-six-year-old woman who lay in a coma in the hospital bed.

The sound—was it a whisper?—came again. This time I could see the colorless lips move.

Holding my breath, I edged forward in the wobbly plastic chair. I was ready to jump to my feet and run. I had better find Mom and Grandma. Great-grandmother Sarah was waking up.

I stretched out a hand to the edge of her bed, steadying myself. Slowly and quietly I began to rise.

Suddenly Sarah's deep brown eyes opened and she stared at me. Her knobby fingers clamped around my wrist so tightly that it hurt.

"Don't go, Anne." It sounded like an order. In a voice as raspy as a fingernail on a blackboard, she managed to utter, "I have something important to tell you."

I took a deep breath, my pounding heart banging loudly in my ears. "I—I'm not my mom—that is, Anne," I stammered. "It's—Lia. Anne's daughter. Mom's down in the hospital cafeteria with Grandma. They asked me to sit with you. Mom and I came to San Francisco because you've been in a coma, and . . ."

I knew I was babbling and it felt as if, as usual, I was doing everything all wrong. I begged, "If you'll let go of me I'll run and get Mom. Grandma, too."

But Sarah didn't seem to hear. Her gaze didn't waver as she stared into my eyes. "Be quiet, Anne," she insisted. "Listen to me."

I realized that Great-grandmother hardly knew me, so I didn't blame her for not recognizing me. But I didn't look like Mom. I didn't look like Grandma. I didn't look the way I was supposed to look at all.

I thought of the long line of strong women from whom I had descended. Tall, big-boned, and handsome, with dark hair and brown eyes, my maternal ancestors had stepped into the world with pride and courage and had accomplished amazing things.

Then there was me.

I couldn't count how often I'd heard Grandma Augusta say, "Speak up, Lia, so people can hear you. And for goodness' sakes get that hair out of

2

your eyes. It looks like you're hiding behind a curtain."

Sometimes Grandma would sigh dramatically, sadly shake her head, and say to my mother, "Look at the child, Anne. She's no bigger than a minute and all that pale hair—where did it come from? She's not a bit like any of the women in our family. If I hadn't been on hand at the hospital when she was born, I might start believing in changelings."

My mom wasn't as blunt, but sometimes she agreed with Grandma. "It's good to be a reader, but, Lia, your nose is *always* in a book. Don't you want to *do* things? You need to meet people. Have more fun."

I always gave the same answer, wondering if Mom would even notice. "I *am* having fun. Reading is fun."

"You're fifteen. You need to have friends."

"I have a friend. A best friend. Jolie."

"I mean lots of friends so you can do some fun things."

"Why should I have lots of friends? I like being with Jolie."

Periodically Grandma and Mom would get so stirred up they'd start a What to Do About Lia project. I'd be signed up for lessons. The worst of all was when they wanted me to go to cheerleading camp. I found it easier to just go along, pay no attention to the other kids—who took the classes with great enthusiasm—and keep doing my own, untalented best. Within two or four weeks the lessons would be over and Jolie and I could go back to exploring the unlimited wonders of our Metairie, Louisiana, branch library. We'd have sleepovers at which we'd read awesome and horrifying ghost stories to each other.

My great-grandmother Sarah's grip on my arm weakened, and she lay back against her pillow. Her eyelids, like brittle, yellowed paper, slowly slid shut. "I have to let you know about Graymoss, Anne," she said. "And I haven't much time or energy to speak—listen to me."

Not knowing what else to do, I muttered, "I'm listening." With a scared, sick feeling, I faced the fact that there might not be time to go for Mom.

"You *do* know about Graymoss, don't you?" Sarah asked. Her eyelids fluttered open again, and she looked as if she were begging me to answer yes.

"Graymoss. Yes, I know a little about it," I replied.

Actually, I'd discovered the existence of Graymoss two years before, when I was thirteen and I had been looking through some old family albums. I'd held up a pencil sketch of a large, graceful two-story house with verandas upstairs and down. Its roof was supported by rows of tall, white Ionic columns.

"What's this place in the picture?" I asked Mom. "The one where someone's written at the bottom 'Graymoss Plantation, 1831.' "

Mom had leaned over my shoulder to study the sketch. "Graymoss was the Blevinses' plantation home. That date must refer to the year it was built," she said.

"This is where the famous Charlotte Blevins

4

lived!" I said. I'd been told often about Charlotte Blevins—my great-great-great—who had lived on Graymoss plantation as a child with her parents and grandparents. In 1861, during the War Between the States, Charlotte's parents and grandmother died. Later, when Charlotte was only sixteen, a detachment of the Union Army marched through that part of Louisiana, looting and burning many of the large plantation houses. Charlotte's grandfather was killed, but somehow Charlotte was able to persuade a Union officer to spare her home. It wasn't burned or destroyed like most in the area.

Charlotte proceeded to grow up and establish a school to teach former slaves and their children to read and write. She was a strong-minded, courageous woman who headed a long line of strong-minded, courageous women.

"What happened to Graymoss after the Civil War?" I'd asked.

Mom had shrugged. "I have no idea. Like many of those old plantations, it probably deteriorated years ago."

I never liked that answer. It didn't satisfy me. In my mind I visualized a deeply green lawn rolling from the back veranda down to the Mississippi River, like the lawns at Oak Alley and some of the other well-kept plantation houses. Graymoss would be a quiet, peaceful place with big rocking chairs on the veranda, and when a light breeze blew, it would ruffle the pages of the book I was reading.

I waited for Sarah to continue with her words about Graymoss. I realized that if anyone in the

5

family knew the answer to my question about the fate of Graymoss, she'd be the one. I asked abruptly, "Great-grandmother, what happened to Graymoss?"

Sarah shuddered, and a strange, fearful look came into her eyes. She took a deep breath and seemed to be trying to gather strength, but her voice wavered as she answered, "Graymoss is there. It's waiting."

My heart jumped. "You mean it? Really? Graymoss is still standing?"

Sarah closed her eyes again, but she continued to speak rapidly. "Listen to me, Anne. I'm leaving Graymoss to you and not to Augusta. Augusta is headstrong and adamant about what should be done with Graymoss. If Augusta had her way Graymoss would be torn down. I can't let that happen. My attorney understands the provisions of Charlotte's will . . . and mine. We must continue to protect the house . . . and care for it. We have no choice."

Sarah's voice grew so low and soft that I had to lean close to hear her.

"Someone has actually cared for the house all these years?" I asked.

"Yes. There is a trust that takes care of taxes, repairs, expenses, and the caretaker's salary."

"I don't understand," I told her. "If the house is still standing and is in good condition, then why hasn't anyone in the family ever lived in it?"

Sarah sighed. Her lips barely moved as she said, "Read Charlotte's diary. Then you'll know."

"Know *what*, Great-grandmother? What will I know?"

6

"Read the diary."

"Where is the diary? Where will I find it?"

For just an instant Sarah's fingers tightened on my arm. "We must save Graymoss, but stay far away from it," she said. "The house is haunted by a terrible, fearful evil."

# CHAPTER TWO

The door opened, and a nurse hurried into the room. "Move back, please," she told me. "Quickly!"

Sarah's fingers had gone limp, so I easily slid my arm from under her hand. Tripping, scrambling to one side, and dragging the chair with me, I managed to end up wedged into a corner near the door.

Another nurse arrived, pushing her way past Mom and Grandma, who had also arrived and were trying to get through the door at the same time.

"What happened?" Mom asked, her voice rising.

The first nurse turned to look at Mom. Then the nurse began turning off things and unfastening some of the tubes that had been attached to

Sarah. "I'm sorry, Mrs. Starling," she said. Then she nodded sympathetically at Grandma. "Mrs. Moore, there's no longer a pulse . . . no heartbeat."

Mom's mouth opened and shut and opened again, but nothing came out. It was the only time I'd seen her at a loss for words.

Grandma's voice broke as she whispered, "We didn't have a chance to say a last goodbye." A tear rolled down Grandma Augusta's cheek, and I felt a terrible wave of sorrow. I shuddered to think how awful it would be, no matter how old you were, to lose your mother, and Sarah was Grandma's mother.

"I'd hoped she'd wake," Grandma Augusta said. She pulled a tissue from the pocket of her skirt and blew her nose loudly.

"She did," I said.

Mom and Grandma turned to look at me.

"What did you say?" Grandma boomed. "Speak up, Lia. This is no time to whisper."

I cleared my throat and took a step away from the corner. "I said—"

"Push your hair out of your eyes and tell us what happened."

Tucking my hair behind my ears, I cleared my throat again and said, "Great-grandmother *did* wake up." I looked at Mom. "She thought I was you, Mom. She kept calling me Anne."

Mom got this disappointed, hurt expression on her face. "Why didn't you come and get us, Lia?"

"I couldn't." I tried to explain. "She was holding my wrist."

Grandma rolled her eyes. Then she reached

down and stroked Sarah's hand. "I see. She was stronger than you?"

The sarcasm in her words made me wince. "Yes," I said. "She was."

Mom sighed. "Lia, dear, why didn't you press the call button for the nurse?"

"I didn't think of it," I whispered.

"She wanted to say goodbye," Mom murmured, and she hugged Grandma.

One of the nurses, nudging and patting, managed to shoo us out of Sarah's room and across the hallway into a small waiting room. "The doctor will be here soon," she explained. "We'll have some papers for you to sign."

As soon as the nurse left, I managed to find the courage to say, "Great-grandmother didn't want to say goodbye. She wanted to talk about Graymoss."

"About Graymoss?" Mom looked surprised. "Was she hallucinating, Lia?"

"No," I said. "She told me about the house, Mom. She said it was waiting."

"That plantation house is still standing? It must be in terrible condition," Mom said.

Grandma frowned and seemed uncomfortable. "I'm sorry Mother said anything about Graymoss. It's a nasty place. When you were young and impressionable, Anne, I made Mother promise not to mention it to you."

"Why?" Mom asked. Suddenly I felt uncomfortable watching my mother in the role of daughter.

"Because it's not far from my home in Baton Rouge, so you'd insist on seeing the house. You know how curious you are. You'd have gone there, no matter what I said. You have to admit you would have."

"Why shouldn't I have seen the house?" Mom asked. She still sounded bewildered. "We could have visited Graymoss together." Her eyes narrowed as she looked at Grandma. "You've visited Graymoss without me, haven't you?"

"I did. Once," Grandma admitted. "Once was enough. But it doesn't matter, does it, because now it will be torn down, as it should have been years ago."

I don't know where I got the courage to say what had happened, but I did. "Great-grandmother said that Graymoss *can't* be torn down. It has something to do with Charlotte Blevins's will. Graymoss isn't in terrible condition. All these years it has had a caretaker."

"What? Did you know about this, Mother?" Mom asked Grandma, almost accusingly.

"Of course I knew," Grandma said.

Mom slowly shook her head. "I still can't imagine why you wouldn't tell me."

"I had to keep you away from the house because . . . well, because it's evil."

Mom gave a surprised laugh as if she couldn't believe what she'd just heard. "An evil house? That doesn't sound like you, Mother. You've never been afraid of anyone or anything—human or beastie. 'We don't believe in ghosts,' you used to tell me. But now you're talking about an evil house?"

Grandma looked down at her lap. Her face was red, and little veins stood out in her forehead. "I know it sounds foolish," she began, "and I don't expect you to believe me—"

She looked so miserable that I interrupted. "I believe you, Grandma," I said. "Because Great-grandmother said the very same thing. She said to take care of the house and protect it, but stay away from it because it was evil."

The spark came back into Grandma's eyes and she raised her head. "There! You see!" she crowed. "When all the legal folderol is over and the house is passed on to me, I'll put an end to it, no matter what Charlotte requested. I'll burn the fool house down."

"You can't," I told her, and now it was my turn to blush as Grandma and Mom stared at me in amazement.

"What I mean is," I told them, "Graymoss won't be yours, Grandma. Great-grandmother Sarah told me she left the plantation to Mom."

I sat through the memorial service for my great-grandmother Sarah Langley, trying not to fidget and wishing I could feel even a little sorrow at her passing.

The minister's talk was filled with high praise for Sarah. He glowed as he described her great courage in ferrying planes from the United States to England during World War II. He glanced at the bronze memorial urn holding Sarah's ashes and spoke in awed tones about her also risking her life to fly medical supplies into Alaskan villages and participating in a daring rescue of two mountain climbers, stranded during a blizzard.

12

I knew all that. I'd heard the stories over and over from Mom. It was Sarah herself I'd never gotten to know. Busy making news and winning awards until she grew too old to travel, she'd had no time to spend in Louisiana with a young great-granddaughter.

I stopped listening to the minister and designed an imaginary banner. Across a bright blue background were gold letters in an elegant script: WOMEN WHO ARE EXCEPTIONALLY BRAVE. I hung it across the back of the chapel, mentally pinning it to the dark red velvet drapes that covered the wall.

Sarah had been brave, and so had her mother, Elizabeth Clary. Elizabeth didn't try to escape San Francisco during the great earthquake of 1906, but helped dig people out of collapsed buildings and save them from the fires that followed.

I suppose everyone took it for granted that Elizabeth had been an exceptionally brave woman. Elizabeth, born in 1877, was Charlotte Blevins's daughter.

Grandmother Augusta was no slouch, either. An army nurse and officer, Augusta helped to arrange rescue operations to get children out of Vietnam. And in the sixties she marched through the South with civil rights groups.

Mom marched with her, when she was a teenager like me. And when Mom got her Ph.D. in psychology, she married Dad because the two of them not only fell in love, but they also had the same dream—to help homeless children. Dad got a job with a child protective agency, and Mom with a private group that counsels abused women

13

and children. They regularly lobbied state and national officials, trying to get funds and better legislation, and Mom had a reputation for not being afraid to tackle anybody—including the President of the United States.

Sighing, I began to embroider names on my imaginary banner, WOMEN WHO ARE EXCEPTIONALLY BRAVE: Charlotte Blevins Porter, Elizabeth Porter Clary, Sarah Clary Langley, Augusta Langley Moore, and Anne Moore Starling. I ran out of space on the banner, but that was all right. There was no way my name could belong on it.

Mom nudged me, and I realized that the minister had stopped speaking and people were leaving the chapel. Augusta began briskly shaking hands with people and thanking them for coming. Mom, too.

I hung back, as I usually did. None of these people wanted to talk to me.

It was surprising how fast the room cleared. I guess everyone was in a hurry. Maybe that was the way things were in San Francisco.

It wasn't like that in Louisiana. As soon as word got out that Grandpa had died, people began coming by Grandma's house with pies and cakes. I'd stayed out of the kitchen because people I'd never seen before were busy sliding casseroles into the oven, and slicing hams, and setting out Grandma's good china plates. After the funeral the house was crowded with people. They cried a little and laughed a lot, telling and retelling stories about Grandpa. Some of the stories got kind of boring, but at least Grandma didn't have to feel alone.

Thinking about Grandpa made me miss him. I

14

was only ten when he died, but I remembered him as being a kind, gentle, quiet man who read stories to me any time I asked.

"Come on, Lia. It's time to go," Mom said.

When I saw that Grandma was carrying the urn with Sarah's ashes in it I took a step back. "Doesn't that urn go to—uh—a cemetery or something?" I asked.

"No," Grandma said. "I'm going to take it home and keep it in the library."

I shuddered. I couldn't help it.

Mom gave one of her impatient sighs and said, "We've got a tight schedule. We have an appointment with Sarah's attorney in an hour. I'd suggest that we have lunch before we meet Mr. Clayton."

"Somewhere with quick service," Grandma added.

I thought of taking the urn into a fast-food hamburger place and started to giggle. The giggle hopped out of control and spread into a belly laugh. I laughed so hard I bent over, holding my stomach. But at the same time I thought of this great-grandmother I didn't really know and how everybody praised her but nobody seemed to be mourning her, and tears for Sarah ran down my face.

Mom wrapped her arms around me and held me tightly. "Darling," she murmured, "I didn't realize what stress all of this has been. I shouldn't have brought you with me."

My sobs and laughter stuck in my throat, turning into hiccups. "It's okay, Mom," I managed to say. "Could I get a drink of water?"

A pale-faced man in a dark suit suddenly ap-

15

peared at my side and held out a glass of water. Gratefully I took it and gulped it down.

Grandma fixed her gaze on the man and asked, "Is there somewhere nearby where we can get food quickly?"

He nodded. "There's a hamburger place on the corner."

I didn't mean to, but once again I exploded into laughter.

"It happens," the man said. "Nervous tension." He shoved an open bottle of smelling salts under my nose, and the horrible smell made me choke and cough. At least it stopped the laughter.

Mom pulled out a tissue and mopped at my eyes.

Grandma said, "I swear she isn't like the Moore side of the family—or anyone else as far back as we know."

Mom patted me reassuringly, and we left the funeral home. As we climbed into our rental car Mom glanced at Sarah's urn. Her eyebrows rose, as they sometimes did when she'd just had a surprising thought, and a tiny smile flickered at the corners of her lips. She said, "Why don't we order at the drive-in window? I saw a small park in the next block. We can eat our hamburgers there."

That was the difference between Mom and me. Mom and I saw the same problem. I had an embarrassing case of hysterics, but Mom worked out a solution to the problem. I slumped down in the backseat, wishing I'd gotten even a few of the genes from the Women Who Are Exceptionally Brave. Why did I get left out?

16

We made it to the office of Gerald R. Clayton, attorney-at-law, exactly on time. It didn't surprise me. Mom and Grandma were always prompt.

Mr. Clayton was a tall, very thin man, who was wearing a charcoal gray pin-striped suit that made him look even thinner. He came to the waiting room to greet us and led us down a hallway to a small conference room. "That was a lovely memorial service for Sarah," he murmured.

When we were all seated and the receptionist had placed glasses of ice water for each of us on the table, Mr. Clayton said, "Sarah was a remarkable woman. Did she tell you that she gave me flying lessons?"

He went on to tell us about the flying club Sarah had founded. It was an exclusive club with high dues, but the dues went to provide summer camp for children who wouldn't have been able to go.

I wished I had gotten to know my great-grandmother. I wished she'd had time to know me. I felt certain that I would have liked her even if her accomplishments seemed overwhelming.

Grandma impatiently shifted in her chair. She cleared her throat, and Mr. Clayton changed the subject. "How long will you be in San Francisco?" he asked.

"Only as long as it takes to dispose of Mother's things," Grandma answered. "Then I'll return to my home in Baton Rouge."

Mr. Clayton nodded, then looked at the papers

in front of him. "Are you ready for me to read the will now?"

"If that's what should be done. Yes," Grandma said.

"It's not a complicated will," Mr. Clayton began. "If you'd like, I can skip all the legal statements in the beginning and summarize it for you. I'll give you a copy to read later."

"Thank you, that will be fine," Grandma agreed. She settled back in her chair to listen.

"Sarah Langley made some provisions for special gifts to a few select friends as well as her long-time caregiver. She has left a donation to the summer camp program, her favorite charity. And now for the family. She has left you, Mrs. Moore, as her only child, her house, most of the furnishings and property within it, and her stocks and bonds."

Grandma nodded. She threw a quick glance at me, as though challenging what I'd told her, and said, "And Graymoss, of course."

"Indeed, she has left property called Graymoss, which consists of a house, all its contents, the outbuildings, and land, to her granddaughter, Anne Starling."

Grandma sat upright, clenching her hands. She stared into Mr. Clayton's eyes. "Are you sure my mother knew what she was doing when she made that provision to her will?"

Mr. Clayton didn't look surprised. I wondered if Sarah had warned him how Grandma would react. He stared right back and said, "This will was dated ten years ago. If you are concerned about whether or not Sarah was of sound mind, I can assure you that she was."

Grandma thought for just a few seconds, then gave in. "It doesn't matter who inherits Graymoss," she said with a voice of authority, "as long as the house is destroyed."

Mr. Clayton picked up the will, turned a page, and continued, "Graymoss comes with a few strings. It was Charlotte Blevins Porter's wish that the house be kept standing and well cared for, and it was important to the dear departed that this wish be carried out to the letter of the law."

"A wish is nothing more than a foolish notion," Grandma retorted. "It wouldn't be binding by law."

"Graymoss has been left to Mrs. Anne Starling conditionally," the lawyer reiterated. "That means she must—"

"We know what *conditionally* means," Grandma snapped. "Just what are these conditions?"

"That Graymoss must continue to be cared for," Mr. Clayton answered. "If Mrs. Starling can't agree to this, then possession of the house and property passes to Mrs. Starling's daughter, Lia Starling, to be held in trust for her until her twenty-fifth birthday."

I started in surprise. "To me? Graymoss?" I could see myself in my daydream again, rocking and reading on the quiet veranda. "Wow!" I whispered to myself.

"That's ridiculous! The house *must* be destroyed!" Grandma insisted.

"Wait a minute," Mom interrupted. I could tell

she'd been thinking hard, because her eyes were wide. "Graymoss is a large place. About how many rooms, would you guess?"

"What has the number of rooms got to do with anything?" Grandma asked.

"It has to do with making a dream come true! If the house is in good condition, or can be repaired without too much expense, I know what we must do."

I sucked in my breath. I knew Mom's dream, and I didn't like it one little bit.

Grandma said, "If you're talking about that notion you and Derek have of adopting a houseful of what are considered unadoptable children—"

"That's exactly what I'm talking about!" Mom exclaimed, grinning and clapping her hands like a little kid. I was embarrassed, but she didn't seem to care.

"But you can't, Anne! I told you, Graymoss is evil!"

Mr. Clayton raised an eyebrow and looked at Grandma as if she'd just claimed there were UFOs on the roof. "Evil? You have firsthand knowledge of some kind of evil?"

Grandma turned red. She looked down at her hands and said, "This is very complicated—it's family business."

"I don't believe in ghosts," Mom said firmly. "But I do believe in trying to bring happiness to as many children as possible."

I groaned. I could see what was going to happen. The quiet rooms, the peaceful veranda—forget it. Graymoss was going to be filled with a crowd of noisy kids for Mom and Dad to care for.

"I can't wait to call Derek and tell him the news," Mom said.

Mr. Clayton broke in. "Don't rush into anything," he said. "There's one more condition to meet. Before you agree to accept Graymoss you must read Charlotte Blevins's diary."

Grandma looked smug. "The diary. That's right. Read it, and you'll soon change your mind about wanting to live in that house. All the others did."

"The others?"

"Elizabeth, Sarah, and even Charlotte herself. Why do you think none of the women in our family ever resided in Graymoss?"

"Because they were scared?" I asked. The mental banner I'd created for the Women Who Are Exceptionally Brave began to fray. I didn't mind.

Grandma frowned at me. "Not *scared*, merely sensible."

Mom looked at Mr. Clayton. "Have you read Charlotte's diary?"

"No, I haven't," he answered. "I am in possession of it now, but the contents of the diary are private."

"It's private because it tells of the terrible evil within the house," Grandma said.

Mr. Clayton held out a book covered in padded cloth. Once it must have had a flower pattern in bright colors, but now it was faded, and there were ragged threads at the edges.

Mom didn't move, but suddenly I found myself standing up. I reached across the desk and took the diary from Mr. Clayton.

Maybe it was because I wasn't like the other

women in the family. Or maybe it was because I read. Or maybe it was because I did believe in ghosts. I sat back down in my chair, the book in my hands, and I shivered with excitement.

I planned to read the diary before Mom ever got a chance to, so that she couldn't tell me not to read it. If there really was evil in Graymoss, I wanted to find out where it had come from. In fact, I hoped to become acquainted with the ghosts that haunted the plantation. Someday, when I was grown, the quiet, peaceful Graymoss—ghosts and all—would be mine.

# CHAPTER THREE

I had plenty of time to read Charlotte's diary. Mom kept arguing with Grandma about the future of Graymoss, and talking on the phone to Dad. No one was the least bit concerned about where I was or what I was doing, so I found a hideaway in Great-grandmother's house—an upstairs sewing room that probably hadn't been used for anything but storage for years and years. I pulled an old quilt off a Boston rocker, settled down, and began to read.

The first part of Charlotte's diary detailed the horrors of the War Between the States, and then Charlotte poured out her heart about how much she missed her parents and grandmother. She wrote a great deal about her grandfather, Placide Blevins, who must have been kind and good to her, because she loved him very much. He liked to read aloud from his most cherished book: *Favorite Tales of Edgar Allan Poe*. He read it so often to Charlotte that the two of them had practically memorized the stories.

Charlotte wrote in her diary:

*I have often wondered, What kind of a man was Edgar Allan Poe who could create such strange, frightening tales?*

*Grandfather told me that Poe's poetry and stories came from a tortured soul and someday I'd understand.*

*Perhaps I will. But for now I'm content to read Poe's stories simply for the pleasurable excitement they stir within my heart and mind.*

"Oh, Charlotte! You loved to read, too!" I said aloud. I felt close to this relative who shared her own love of books with me by providing me with her own diary to read.

As I read, it became obvious to me how very much the Graymoss plantation meant to Charlotte. She had been born in Graymoss. She loved the beauty of her home and described the ornate ceilings with special moldings that were full of designs with swirls and flowers, yet looked like eyes and mouths and even noses of strange people and animals if the light was dim.

*I love to use my imagination, too,* I thought, delighted that I'd discovered an ancestor so much like myself.

Charlotte wrote about her best friend, Lenci Cavanaugh, but there was very little about games or boys, because the miseries of the War Between the States dominated their lives. The Blevinses and Cavanaughs had field hands who had run away, heading north to freedom, so everyone had to pitch in and help since crops still had to be planted and harvested, although most of the vegetables and fruit they'd grown had been taken by army troops to feed the soldiers.

Charlotte's grandfather was desperate for help and hired a foreman, Morgan Slade. Charlotte renamed Mr. Slade the Cat.

*He sneaks in and out of the house as quietly as a cat slips through an open window. His eyes dart from one side to the other with a glitter to them, yet he never misses a thing. I suspect him of snooping around our house. I wouldn't put it past him. When Grandfather isn't nearby Mr. Slade is mean to the workers. I've heard him yell and curse them if he finds something not to his liking. Grandfather must have heard about this from someone because he has had words with Mr. Slade. It hasn't helped. Mr. Slade is even more surly. I know that Grandfather is desperate for hired help, so he hasn't fired Mr. Slade. I wish he could because I don't trust Mr. Slade.*

There were breaks in Charlotte's diary, and the entries grew shorter.

*I can't help worrying how we will manage to survive, although Grandfather keeps assuring me that things will turn out all right eventually. He insists they always do.*

I worried along with Charlotte as I read her diary. As the South suffered great losses, Charlotte grew even more fearful about the future. Food be-

25

came scarcer. I ached for Charlotte as she described her sixteenth birthday:

*The day began happily. After we had breakfasted, Grandfather took me to a lovely spot in the side yard that was mottled with sun and shade. He knew I had long wished for an herb garden, so he had made and planted one for me. Thyme, dill, rosemary—all were bordered with a graceful brick edging. Grandfather had helped to build Graymoss, so I knew how much he loved to work with brick and mortar. Sharing his talents with me had been a real labor of love, and I was delighted with his gift.*

*Later, Grandfather came in with a hen—one that had escaped the last group of foragers by running into the woods. The bird looked old enough to be tough, but Grandfather and I cleaned and plucked it and baked it slowly for two hours in half a bottle of his best white wine. With a bouquet of wildflowers on the table, the candelabra filled with glowing candles, and the chicken on a platter, I could ignore the usual turnips and boiled potatoes that accompanied the chicken and call the dinner a birthday feast.*

*Mr. Slade suddenly appeared. Greedily eying the chicken, he bluntly said that he wanted to share the meal, but Grandfather respected my wishes and told him we were having a private family dinner.*

*Mr. Slade eyed the silver candelabra and smiled. "It won't be long now until the Federals march in," he said. "Those fancy candlesticks and the rest of your silver will make pretty souvenirs—that is, if they're still here when the Federals arrive."*

*"What do you mean by that, sir?" Grandfather demanded.*

*"I mean those valuables could set a man up for a better*

26

life—one in which he wouldn't be turned away from a dinner table because he wasn't good enough."

"Are you threatening me?"

"I'm just making a point, so to speak," Mr. Slade said, and his narrowed cat eyes swept the room, coming to rest once more on the candelabra. "You—with your elegant house and fancy furniture and rows of expensive wines in your fine cellar—might not understand how a man with a simple life might feel. Someone like me should be treated with respect, too. . . ."

I was shocked and horrified at Mr. Slade's rudeness. "This is my birthday dinner, sir," I told him. "It's my own wish that my Grandfather and I share it in private."

The cat eyes turned on me as he smiled. It wasn't a pleasant smile. It was so evil that I trembled. "Be careful, Miss," he said. "You're a treasure, too, and when men are at war anything is fair game."

"That's enough, Mr. Slade," Grandfather ordered. "Please leave this house." Grandfather's eyes blazed as he watched Mr. Slade saunter out of the room.

With gallantry Grandfather seated me and filled my plate. It was difficult, but we pretended nothing unpleasant had happened and we were having a lovely celebration.

I am afraid of Mr. Slade. He surely doesn't mean us well. Now I fear he'll do exactly as he threatened and steal everything of value in our house. How should we protect ourselves against him? I can't think of a single way to do so.

I dropped the book to my lap and grumbled aloud, "Morgan Slade, you were a rat!" But I picked up the diary again. I had to find out what happened.

There was another, longer break in the diary. Charlotte's next entry upset me more.

*Today was one of the worst days in my life. Old Glen Harper, who works on the Robeson plantation upriver, rode by to tell us that the Union Army was on its way.*

*I saw Mr. Harper arrive, his horse all in a lather. I had been working in the vegetable garden, and I came running up to the house. I knew something must be wrong. Grandfather sent Mr. Harper on his way to warn others, then told me the news.*

*"What shall we do?" I cried.*

*Grandfather wrapped his arms around me and held me tightly. "We knew the army would be coming," he said. "Don't be afraid. I'm here to take care of you."*

*I realized his coat was torn at the shoulder, and the sleeve and front were spotted with a white powder. I stepped back to take a good look at him and saw a bruise on his cheek. "What happened to you?" I asked.*

*"Slade attacked me," Grandfather said. "He was running away and taking our family valuables with him. Your mother's jewelry was in his pocket, and he carried a bag with the silver, too. The last thing he said to me was that he, and not I, would enjoy what remained of my wine."*

*Grandfather paled, and I felt him tremble. "Slade intended to take you, too, Charlotte," he said quietly and shook his head sadly. But his eyes looked determined.*

*I gasped in fear, but Grandfather stroked my hair back from my forehead and murmured, "Dear little granddaughter, I would not allow anything so vile to happen to you. Slade and I came to an understanding. He can keep the valuables—they are of no real importance—and he will not harm you."*

*I felt physically ill at Slade's villainy. As Grandfather*

stepped back, his hands reassuringly on my shoulders, I saw an excited, almost frantic look in his eyes.

"There's a great deal I must tell you," he said. "But not now. With the Federals so close by, it's better if you do not know the answers yet."

"What answers?" I asked. "I don't understand."

Grandfather held out a book to me and said, "Keep this, Charlotte. Take good care of it." It was his book of tales by Edgar Allan Poe.

I stared at the book, familiar with its soft leather binding. The top of a bookmark protruded. Unfortunately, at the time I was not curious enough to open the book and note the page. I said, "You are being very puzzling, Grandfather. I asked you questions, and you gave me only this book as your answer."

"You'll understand soon enough, Charlotte," he explained. "If anything should happen to me . . . well, the answers to your questions are in these pages."

We could hear the thunder of hoofbeats on the road, and I cried out. I dropped the book into a pocket of my apron and clung to Grandfather.

A small detachment of Union Army soldiers raced through our gate and up to the house. These were not professional soldiers in control. They were ragtag, and I fear that a few of them had been drinking. Three of the men waved guns. Some of them yelled and whooped. One held high a burning torch. It was a fearful sight.

"Burn the house!" one of the men shouted.

But the officer in charge held up a hand and reined in his horse. The men stopped their horses behind him. "You, sir," the officer said to Grandfather. "Are you the landowner here?"

"I am," Grandfather said.

"Is there anyone inside your house?"

I couldn't bear to see them burn our home. I have never been so terrified in my life. I burst into tears. Grandfather reached into the inside breast pocket of his coat—for his handkerchief, I am sure—but one of the soldiers raised his gun and fired.

Grandfather clutched his chest and dropped to the ground.

The officer yelled at his men, but I paid him no attention. I rushed to Grandfather, holding him in my arms, trying to lift his head from the sharp gravel on the drive. "Don't die!" I sobbed. "Please don't leave me! I need you, Grandfather!"

"The house," he whispered. "Charlotte, you must—"

His words stopped as blood bubbled up in his throat. Sobbing, I finished what he had wanted to say. "I must save the house. Yes, Grandfather, I will save the house."

Somehow I managed to lay him down gently and climb to my feet. My dress and apron were stained with dirt and blood, but I pulled myself as tall as I could stand and looked into the eyes of the army officer. "You have killed an innocent man who would have done you no harm," I told him. "That was not an act of war. You and your men are nothing better than drunken murderers."

The soldier who had shot Grandfather spoke up. "I thought he was reachin' for a gun."

"My grandfather was the only family I had left," I said to the officer. "You've taken him away from me. Are you going to take my home away, too?"

The officer looked troubled. "How old are you?" he asked.

"I'm sixteen."

"Where are your parents?"

"They were killed in an accident two years ago."

"You have no other relatives?"

"A distant cousin of my mother's who lives in Baton Rouge," I replied.

The worry lines on his face deepened. "This cousin—will she take you in? I have a daughter your age. You can't stay here alone."

I glared at him with all my might, and I hoped he could feel my hatred. "My age doesn't matter," I said. "I will send for my mother's cousin, but until she comes I can do whatever is needed. I beg you to grant me this one reprieve. Do not burn my home, sir. There is nothing valuable inside. That has all been stolen already. Just leave the house standing.

The men looked from me to their officer. I stood still, waiting patiently while he frowned, his anguished thoughts showing on his face.

"Leave the house be. Ride on," he called to his men. He spurred his horse and headed for the road.

Some of the soldiers grumbled their dissatisfaction, but they wheeled their horses and rode after him.

"I hope you are sorry for the horrible crime you have committed," I shouted as a fresh wave of anger boiled up within my heart, but of course they couldn't hear me.

As soon as the men had ridden out of sight I ran to Grandfather, cradled his head in my arms, and cried until dry sobs shook my body and there were no more tears.

Some of our farm help had come out of hiding, waiting patiently until my storm had passed. They moved forward, helping me to rise. They lifted Grandfather's body, carried it into the house, and placed it on his bed.

After what Grandfather had told me, I was desperately afraid of Slade. "Is Mr. Slade gone?" I asked.

"There's been no sign of Mr. Slade since earlier this mornin'," John answered.

"Was he here when Mr. Harper arrived with the news?"

"No'm. As I said, we haven't seen him since this mornin'."

I glanced at the top of Grandfather's dresser. Normally it held a carved wooden box, inlaid with mother-of-pearl. The box was gone. So was the pair of oil lamps with silver and teak bases.

I left the bedroom and walked down the stairs, going from room to room. All the silver was gone, as was the crystal. Heartsick, I realized that Mr. Slade had done just as he had threatened. He'd stolen all our family treasures and mementoes. I hated him all the more.

Upstairs, my mother's jewelry box had vanished, and with it her silver-backed brush, mirror, and comb.

I checked the barn and discovered that Mr. Slade hadn't taken our buggy or his horse. I didn't understand his thinking. All I could deduce was that he had been afraid of meeting up with Union soldiers on the road and had cut through the woods on foot. I sent John to ride to Baton Rouge to inform my mother's cousin, Lydia Hartwell, that Grandfather was dead and I had need of her help.

I went back upstairs, washed Grandfather's body with warm water and soap, and dressed him in his best suit of clothes. Then I washed myself from head to foot and changed into clean clothing. The bloody dress and apron I had worn I threw into the fireplace in my bedroom and lit the kindling to start the fire. Clothing was hard to come by, but I could never wear that dress again.

At the last moment, just as the fabric began to smolder, I remembered the book tucked inside the pocket of my apron. I pulled at a corner of the apron, dragging it from the flames, and quickly tugged the book from its pocket. I tossed the apron back into the fire and stamped out the few sparks that burned on the hearth.

One corner of the book's cover had been singed, and it

smelled of smoke. The bookmark had fallen out and was gone. But I carried the book to the window and looked through it carefully, page by page. I think I had hoped that if Grandfather had meant to give me a message in the book he would have hidden a scrap of paper within its pages. Or perhaps he had underlined words in a type of code. But I could find nothing. Perhaps the page in which the bookmark rested had contained the clue I needed. But through my carelessness I had lost the bookmark and had no way of knowing on which page it had rested.

In the waning light of the day I sat in Grandfather's bedroom with my mother's prayer book open in my hands and tried to pray for Grandfather's soul, as was right and proper. But shadows grew deeper, and the house seemed to be filling with soft and secret sounds. I lit a lamp, then leaned back in the chair, hoping for a few moments of rest and peace. But as I glanced upward, the designs in the molding turned into tiny faces with mean mouths and hard eyes. Unable to look away, I glimpsed sharp teeth and tongues that curled and split like serpents' tongues. A breeze lifted the curtains at the window, hissing frigid air into the room. The little eyes narrowed, and the tongues waggled, whispering words I didn't want to hear. A horrible sense of evil wrapped around me, twisting about my throat.

I tried to breathe, but I was suffocating. I gasped. I panted. With all my strength I clutched the arms of the chair and thrust myself upward, yelling, choking, coughing.

Whatever courage I had was completely gone. Aching with shame, I knew that I would be unable to do the proper thing and sit with Grandfather's body. I couldn't stay in this house alone another minute. I tore down the stairs and out through the back door with whispers twining around my legs and shadowy fingers plucking at my hair and arms.

That night I slept in the barn.

There was more in the diary about Graymoss and about Placide Blevins's funeral and about Cousin Lydia Hartwell, who was a dumpling-shaped, humorless, elderly widow who unenthusiastically and out of duty, according to Charlotte, offered her a home.

*What has happened to Graymoss? In the daylight my home seems as warm and welcoming as it has always been. But at night strange, unearthly things happen. Freezing winds blow through the house, doorknobs rattle and turn, and voices hiss and whisper around me. They are saying something—some word repeated over and over—but I can't make it out. I don't want to. All this is not my imagination. Until Cousin Lydia arrived, I made the barn my sleeping quarters.*

*The few workers who had stayed with our family thought I had become unsettled because of losing Grandfather. They didn't believe me when I told them what I had seen and heard. At their urging, I arranged for Grandfather's immediate burial in the family crypt, hoping that they were right in telling me that soon all the bad feelings in the house would be gone.*

*That night I tried going to bed in the house again, but once more the eyes goggled at me and the mouths opened in whispers, ravings, and screams. I grabbed my quilt and, barefoot, ran to the barn.*

*Amos, the tall, strapping fellow who grooms the horses and drives the carriage, told me that he would prove to me that what I heard and saw was only in my mind. I could stay in the barn that night, and he would sleep in the house.*

*With all my heart I hoped he was right. But it didn't surprise me when not long after nine o'clock Amos flung* the back door open and came tearing down the steps, yelling so loudly that some of the others came running.

Amos shook as he talked and hung on to a fence rail for support. "Miss Charlotte is right! There's somethin' horrible inside that house!" he cried.

"Ghosts?" somebody asked.

"Worse than ghosts," Amos answered. "And there was a voice sayin' somethin'."

"What did it say?" I asked.

"I don't know," Amos said. "I didn't stay long enough to make it out."

Bill and Peter glanced at the house with interest. Peter took a step toward it.

"Don't you try goin' in there, 'less you want your heart scared right out of your body," Amos warned.

But Bill grinned, and Peter laughed. "Mr. Blevins was a good man," Bill said. "We don't expect his ghost to harm us none."

"It's not Grandpa's ghost!" I insisted. "It's something else—an evil, horrible presence."

Bill chuckled. "This is somethin' we gotta see," he said. "Might be a story worth talkin' about for years to come."

He and Peter walked through the open back door of the house and shut it behind them while the rest of us watched.

We didn't have long to wait before they came running out of the house, colliding with each other in the doorway, struggling to escape. Their faces were twisted in fear, and all they could say was, "Amos was right. Stay away from that place."

John arrived the following afternoon with Cousin Lydia in her buggy. She looked the house over and declared that it was a fine specimen of Greek Revival and, if enough good help could be obtained, she wouldn't object at all to moving to Graymoss to live.

I tried to explain about the evil that crept into the house each evening as daylight ended, but it didn't do any good. Lydia was horrified at the idea of sleeping in the barn and insisted on sleeping in the house in a proper bed. I warned her again of what to expect, but she sighed, rolling her eyes. "This is what comes of the books you are reading," she said. "Make-believe tales and stories are not the proper thing for young ladies to put into their impressionable young minds."

She took possession of Poe's book, "for your own good," as she said, and hid it somewhere within the house.

I didn't search for it. In a way I was glad not to have the book near me. It seemed, in some strange way, to be tied into the terror and evil that had taken over Graymoss.

That night, as darkness crept across the land, I lit every candle and lamp within the house, hoping to keep the evil at bay. Lydia scoffed at my "wastefulness," snuffing out as many candles as she could reach. She led the way upstairs, insisting that she had had an exhausting day so we would retire early.

As she reached the third stair from the top, her legs suddenly shot out from under her and she tumbled backward. Bracing myself against the banister, I broke her fall, and we sat on the stairs together, both of us shaking like saplings in a strong wind.

"The lamp!" she cried.

"It's still in your hand," I reassured her. "The oil didn't even spill."

Lydia looked at me strangely. "The stairs are too highly polished. They're slippery."

I shook my head. "They haven't been polished for over a year. We don't have enough help, and I've been working in the fields, so I haven't had time."

Lydia took a couple of deep breaths and pulled herself to

her feet. "Be careful," she said, and led the way to the upstairs hallway, taking one deliberate step at a time. What happened to Lydia to make her fall? I have no idea.

When I reached my bedroom I didn't undress. I didn't even remove my shoes. I sat in the small lady's slipper chair near the fireplace and waited, ready to flee the house. From the next room I could hear Lydia's rhythmic snoring.

Then I began to hear something else. I could hear the whispers curling around the banisters and up the stairway, creeping down the hallway and sliding under the door of my room. The faces in the moldings pinched themselves into shapes that were even more horrifying than before and waggled their split tongues at me. The whispers became words, wrapping around me, but I was too frightened to listen and understand them.

I jumped to my feet just as a horrible scream shook the house. The whispers quivered in the air and withdrew with tiny chuckles, as Lydia slammed open her bedroom door. Racing to join her in the hallway, we nearly collided. She wrapped me in a stranglehold, her eyes so wide and fearful, they were almost rolled back in her head.

"Down the stairs!" I shouted at her, struggling to break from her grasp. "Come with me! Come!"

With the whispers stroking, pulling, and pushing at us, we staggered out the front door and collapsed on the porch.

I waited until Lydia had caught her breath, then said, "Come to the barn with me. We'll sleep on the straw."

Without a word, Lydia followed me.

The next day we packed my belongings and moved to Lydia's home in Baton Rouge.

# CHAPTER FOUR

There wasn't much more to the diary. I found a folded, yellowed sheet of paper tucked between the last pages and opened it. A grown-up Charlotte Blevins Porter had written about hiring a caretaker to keep Graymoss in good condition. Apparently Cousin Lydia had left a sizable amount of money to Charlotte when she died, and Charlotte had added to it from her own income to set up a fund to care for Graymoss.

*I have done my best to discover the answer Grandfather said I would find in* Favorite Tales of Edgar Allan Poe, Charlotte wrote. *But, to my sorrow, I have failed. I do not understand why there is an evil presence in Graymoss. There must be a reason, as there must be a way to get rid of its terrible power. Now and then people have arrived and have tried to send the evil away, but none of them suc-*

*ceeded. Each of them—even a woman well practiced in voodoo magic—has fled the house in terror. Its reputation has spread, and now no one will even go near Graymoss. All I can do is arrange to keep the house as Grandfather had wanted it to be and hope that someday the evil will leave.*

I closed the diary and leaned back in the rocker. "Wow!" I said. "Mom wants to fill Graymoss with kids? She has *got* to read this!"

I tried to be honest. I admitted to myself I was jealous. But was it wrong to want my parents for myself? I'd hate sharing them with a noisy pack of little kids.

It looked as if I wouldn't have to. I couldn't help smiling at the situation of the ghost—or whatever it was—in the house. As far as I was concerned, the yucky old thing was welcome to Graymoss—at least for now. I'd be in my own home in Metairie with Jolie and a stack of good books.

I could hear Mom and Grandma coming up the stairs, so I went to the top landing to meet them.

"I think you and Derek are behaving very foolishly," Grandma was saying, so I was afraid that Mom had won the argument.

"We're simply going to look at the house. That's all," Mom said.

My hopes rose. That was all she needed—just look at the house . . . and the plaster ceiling decorations that turned into horrible faces, and feel the cold winds, and hear the voices whispering . . . Charlotte hadn't told her diary if she'd ever found out the word the voices whispered, but that didn't matter. What mattered was that the ghosts were going to keep Mom and Dad out of Graymoss.

"Hi," I said, and held out the diary. "Mom, you really need to read Charlotte's diary."

Mom looked at her watch. "I will. But later, not now."

"No, now. Really. Before you keep making plans."

Mom was only half listening to me. "We've got so much to clean out here. People save so many, many things." She stopped as she reached the landing and asked, "Have you read all of the diary, Lia?"

"Yes," I answered.

"Good. Then while we're going through Sarah's dresser drawers, why don't you tell me what Charlotte wrote?"

Grandma turned into the large bedroom on the right. Mom followed her, and I trailed behind.

"I think you'd better read it yourself," I said. I was sure that Charlotte's own words would be more effective than any retelling I could do.

Mom pulled out a drawer and began taking out slips and stockings and things and stacking them on the bed. "We can put these into big plastic bags," she told Grandma, "and give them to the Goodwill."

"Mom . . ."

She didn't even look up. "Lia, honey, I told you I haven't got time to read it now. You and I are flying back home tomorrow, and I want to help your grandmother as much as I can before we leave."

40

I sighed and sat on the far edge of the bed. "Okay then. I'll tell you what Charlotte wrote. But don't talk. Just listen."

Mom and Grandma didn't say anything. They just kept shaking things out, looking them over, folding them again, and putting them in stacks.

So I told Mom about Charlotte's grandfather being shot and the foreman disappearing with all the family's valuables. Then I lowered my voice and tried to sound scary as I described Charlotte's first experience with the evil in the house.

As I talked, Mom stopped working and looked at me. Her mouth kind of twisted, and her eyes crinkled, and when I stopped to take a breath, she burst out laughing.

"What's so funny?" I really felt insulted.

"The faces you were making," Mom said. "When you told about the faces in the plaster moldings, you scrunched up your eyes and waggled your tongue."

"I did?"

"Yes, you did." Mom came around the side of the bed and hugged me. "Lia," she said, "you can't possibly believe some silly tale about ghosts."

"Yes, I can," I insisted. "Charlotte wrote about what she saw. And other people saw and heard the same things. Her mother's cousin, for one, and some of their field help, and people who came to get rid of the evil." I pulled the sheet of paper from the diary and handed it to Mom. "Just read this much. Okay?"

Mom did. She handed the paper back to me and smiled. "There may have been some kind of mass hysteria involved," she said. "Or rumors that ev-

41

eryone believed because they wanted to be frightened. I refuse to go along with this silly business about some kind of scary evil because there are no such things as ghosts. We don't believe in them."

"Maybe you and Dad don't, but—"

Mom went on. "In any case, you can see that it was important to Charlotte that the house be well cared for. I can't think of a better way to care for it than to fill it with love and children—children who have been unadoptable and who badly need a home and parents to love them."

Mom's gaze got kind of dreamy. "Once there must have been fields at Graymoss that were productive with crops, and a vegetable garden, and fruit trees, and even a woods. It would take a lot of hard work to put things in order again, but we could give the land new life." She clapped her hands again, which I wished she wouldn't do because it was embarrassing behavior for a woman her age. "Your father is every bit as excited about this as I am," she added.

I glanced over at Grandma, who was tenderly holding a small cameo pin. She had tears in her eyes, and I realized how sad she must be to have lost her mother. For once I was on Grandma's side. "Tell us about the evil, Grandma," I said.

"I told you I experienced it once. Once was enough."

"Then tell Mom just what it was like," I said.

Grandma put the cameo back in the jewelry box. "It makes no difference. Your mother's old enough to do what she wants to, and she and Derek are bound and determined they're going to live in Graymoss."

"But—"

"They'll live there for one night, and that's all," Grandma added. "One night will be enough to change their minds."

I persisted. "Did you hear the whispers or see the faces on the ceiling?"

"It doesn't matter, does it?" Grandma grumbled.

Mom and I were both watching Grandma, and she frowned at us. "Out of curiosity I stayed in the house until it grew dark," she said. "It was then that I felt it."

She stopped, so I asked, "Felt what?"

"The chill, the strangeness, a sudden dimness. A window in the library must have opened because a wind blew through the room. It seemed to wrap around me, and I thought that I heard . . ." She shook her head, as though she were trying to clear her mind of unhappy memories. "Never mind. I don't know what I heard. There's no point in going into details. I ran from the house, jumped into my car, and drove to the nearest town. That's it. Are you satisfied?"

"Well, not exactly, but . . ." I turned to Mom. "Now do you see?"

"I see that my mother read Charlotte's diary and fell under its spell. The things she expected to happen did. It's a classic case of—"

"Mom! Sometimes I wish you weren't a psychologist! You try to make everything fit into a pattern. You don't want to admit there's an evil something haunting Graymoss, but there is!"

Mom laughed again and scooped up an armful of Sarah's things. "Ghosts! Creatures that go bump in the night! Boo! I'm scared!" she said.

"What's the matter with the two of you? Where's the courageous spirit for which the women of our family have always been noted?"

She carried the bundle of clothing downstairs, but her question remained and started me to thinking. "Grandma," I asked, "did your mother ever visit Graymoss?"

Grandma looked away. She seemed embarrassed. "Once or twice," she said.

"Great-grandmother ferried planes during World War Two, and saved somebody in Alaska during a blizzard, but she was afraid of Graymoss?"

"She was sensible," Grandma insisted, and loudly snapped Sarah's jewelry box closed. "Not afraid, sensible."

"How about *her* mother—Elizabeth—who stayed in San Francisco during aftershocks and fires to help people trapped in the great earthquake? Wasn't she brave enough to do something with Graymoss?"

Grandma frowned at me. "Elizabeth was a legend in bravery. If she stayed away from Graymoss, she had a perfectly good reason."

"Charlotte didn't go back, either," I said. "All those brave women—except they were afraid of Graymoss."

"Oh, ho! And I suppose you wouldn't be?" Grandma snapped.

I thought a moment and smiled. "I'd be scared, all right, if what happened to Charlotte happened to me, but I want to see Graymoss, in spite of what's there. I really do."

Mom walked back into the room. "I'm glad to hear you say that, Lia," she said, "because your

44

father and I have planned a visit to Graymoss on Saturday. I'd much rather bring you with us than leave you with Jolie's family. I don't want to impose on the Lynds."

I clutched the diary tightly and hugged it to my chest. I was going to visit the plantation where Charlotte had lived! I was going to find out if what she had written about the evil in the house was true.

And, best of all, I wasn't afraid—at least not runaway afraid of Graymoss like the Women Who Are Exceptionally Brave in our family—because I planned to go to the house prepared. First I would swear Jolie to secrecy. Then Jolie and I would search the Metairie Public Library for books that would tell us how to deal with ghosts.


Mom read Charlotte's diary in the plane on the way home. I watched her face, hoping for some sign of alarm or worry or fear. But her expression didn't change. When she had finished reading, I clutched her arm. "Well? What do you think now about Graymoss?"

"I'm so excited I want to sing and dance and jump up and down—right here on this plane," Mom said.

I groaned and looked around quickly, hoping no one had heard her. I leaned closer, lowering my voice. "Cut it out, Mom," I said. "I mean really. What do you really think?"

"I really am excited," Mom said. "The interior of the house must be beautiful, with large rooms and high ceilings. And I can't wait to see if the building itself is structurally sound. You've seen the drawing—the wide verandas, the tall columns. Oh, Lia! What a wonderful gift my grandmother has given me. Your Dad and I can carry out our dream."

It was difficult to keep back the tears. "What about me?" I demanded. "I'm part of this family, too, aren't I? You know what *I* think about moving away from Jolie and living in a place full of kids. I told you when you and Dad were first talking about what you'd like to do *someday*."

"Oh, honey," Mom said, "you may not realize it now, but you'll be enthusiastic, too, when you discover how wonderful a big family can be."

"A big family in a haunted house," I muttered.

Mom patted my hand as though I were five years old. "Lia, dear, I see why Charlotte's writings found a receptive audience in you. You *want* the house to be unlivable."

"No, I don't. Well, yes, I do. I mean—"

Mom went on. "Charlotte must have been highly imaginative, just as you are. Remember—she said she liked to pretend to see faces in the moldings?"

"She couldn't have imagined all that she described."

"Couldn't she? She had just had a traumatic experience in seeing her beloved grandfather shot. Her parents had died, so they weren't on hand to provide stability for her. Her cousin Lydia wasn't the least bit sympathetic or lovable. Charlotte was vulnerable, so her overactive imagination took control."

I shook my head. "Then what about the workers who saw and heard what she did?"

"That's easy," Mom said. "The power of suggestion."

"Her cousin Lydia was terrified."

Mom nodded. "I know. But what I *don't* know was how much of the sounds and sights that frightened the poor woman were generated—probably unconsciously—by Charlotte herself."

I grumpily folded my arms across my chest and slid down in my seat. "You have an answer for everything, don't you?"

Mom was silent for a few minutes. Then she asked, "Lia, do you really want Graymoss to be 'haunted'?"

I could feel my face turn red. Of course I wanted Graymoss to be haunted. I wanted it to be filled with scary and weird things. I wanted Mom and Dad and me to go back to our home in Metairie and leave Graymoss alone—at least until I was grown.

But I couldn't tell Mom that. Instead, I muttered, "That's a crazy question."

"I've talked about the dream your father and I have had for a long time, and I guess I've taken it for granted that you're a part of that dream. Maybe I haven't paid attention when you've made negative comments. I just assumed that you'd come around to our way of thinking when we eventually were able to provide a home for kids no one has wanted to adopt."

"How many kids are we talking about?"

"At least a dozen. More, I hope. Eventually two

dozen. I've talked to the right people about the idea, and if we just had the proper environment for the children—"

I tried another argument against the idea. "It costs a lot to raise children. You'd have to be a millionaire to have enough food and clothing for so many."

Mom smiled. "There are government funds for adoptive parents of hard-to-place children. It's possible that we could use those. With the legacy that comes with Graymoss and the income from Dad's job, we could swing it."

My feelings spilled over, and I blurted out, "A dozen kids running and yelling and fighting and tearing up things. You'd spend all your time with them."

I could hear the disappointment in Mom's voice. "The children wouldn't be out of control. I'd be there to supervise, to set rules and boundaries, and to help them develop social skills . . . and, most of all, to give them some of the love and care they need. Just what I do for you."

I didn't have to answer, because two flight attendants stopped at our row with their cart and everyone got busy.

Was I so wrong because I wanted a normal life like everyone else? The food that was served sat in front of me. I bit into my sandwich, but the over-sized bun was dry and tough and hard to swallow.


I wanted to read Charlotte's diary again, so Mom let me borrow it. I planned to read it—but only after Jolie had. Jolie came over. I told her what

Mom and Dad wanted to do with Graymoss. Then I gave her the diary to read while we sat in my room. I fidgeted and squirmed while she made little noises at the scary parts, twisting her longish blond hair back and forth.

Finally, after she'd read the entire diary, she stared at me with wide eyes and asked, "Are you really going to Graymoss on Saturday? Really?"

"Really," I answered.

Jolie sighed. "I'd be too scared."

"I didn't say I wasn't scared of what might be in that house," I admitted. "But I do want to find out."

"What if . . . what if the evil that hides there and comes out at night harms you?"

"I'll protect myself."

"Protect yourself against a ghost? How?"

"That's what I have to find out," I said.

"What if the evil thing hurts you first? Even kills you?" Jolie asked.

"It can't. Ghosts can scare, but they can't kill people."

"Yes, they can," Jolie said. "I read about it. They have records of a ghost that pushed a man over a cliff, and one who disguised himself as a woman's husband and led her into a cave, where she fell into a pit and drowned."

"Ugh! Stop it!" I said, but I thought uncomfortably of Cousin Lydia and her fall on the stairs. Had she been pushed? If Charlotte hadn't caught Lydia, what might have happened to her? I shivered.

"Would you come to the library with me right now?" I said. "Since we're driving to Graymoss on

49

Saturday, I have to learn as much as I can about ghosts before then."

I'd expected Jolie to get excited about the ghost hunt, but instead she looked at me with tears puddling in her eyes and spilling down her cheeks.

"Oh, Lia," she cried, "you're my best friend. I don't want you to move away."

"We won't. When Mom and Dad find out that the house really is haunted by evil, they'll give up their idea."

Jolie's lower lip turned down. "I don't want to lose you."

"You won't lose me," I reassured her.

Jolie nodded, the tears dropping onto her lap and making dark spots on her shorts. "But you'll be in the house while the evil is there. Graymoss isn't haunted by some wispy spirit in a long white dress that floats off when someone gets near," Jolie said. "I read what Charlotte wrote, just like you did. Whatever is in that house is evil and dangerous. The people who ran away from it had good reason."

I'd never seen Jolie so upset. "Calm down," I told her. "The thing in the house isn't going to hurt me."

"Don't be so sure," Jolie said. "Just stay away from it, Lia. I have this awful feeling that I may never see you again!"

# CHAPTER FIVE

Jolie and I set to work at the library's computers, amazed at the number of people who had written about ghosts.

"This one looks good," Jolie said, and wrote down a title. "It's ghost stories to tell around a campfire."

"That's not what we want," I said. "We want something like . . . well, sort of like a specialist would write about how to protect yourself against ghosts."

You mean like *The Exorcist?*"

"That's not what I mean at all. We don't want fiction. We want nonfiction."

"You mean like those books about UFOs landing in New Mexico?"

"No! I mean—" I put my chin in my hands and

said, "I don't know what I mean. What I want is a sort of recipe for what to do about ghosts."

"Okay," Jolie said. "We'll keep looking."

I found a couple of titles and wrote down their call numbers. Jodi found two more, so we went to the stacks to find them. We sat cross-legged on the floor and skimmed through the books.

Of the four books, only three were on hand. Two were simply chapters about visits to haunted houses, with nothing really helpful listed. The third book, however, did tell about the power of evil. The author claimed to be able to withstand ghosts throwing china and knocking over tables through strong mind control.

"Mind control, oh, sure," I said. "Like anybody can have it."

"What is it?" Jolie asked.

"The author doesn't say. Only that she's got it." I sighed. "What am I going to do?"

"Tell your parents you don't want to go with them to Graymoss on Saturday. Stay here with me."

"That's not the kind of advice I need. I need someone who knows how to deal with evil."

Jolie suddenly blinked and sat up straight. "I know who," she said. "One of Mom's friends was telling her all about a voodoo shop in New Orleans. Voodoo. You know. There are all kinds of voodoo spells. They probably have one to get rid of ghosts."

I began to get excited. "Do you know where the voodoo shop is?"

"In the French Quarter," Jolie said. "Mom's friend told her that there are a lot of voodoo shops there. They sell stuff to tourists and to people who still practice voodoo."

I jumped up and shoved the books back where we'd got them. "Let's go home and get some money and ride the commuter into New Orleans."

When we got home Jolie called her mother and told her she'd be with me. I told Mom I was going to be with Jolie. We were telling the truth. Both mothers were so used to our being together, they automatically said okay without asking where we'd be.

"Let's take Charlotte's diary with us," I said. "It will give the people who sell voodoo a better idea of why I need it."

The diary wasn't in sight, so I leaned over the stair railing and yelled downstairs to Mom to ask what had happened to it.

Mom came to the foot of the stairs and quietly said, "I shouldn't have allowed you to read it again. I shouldn't have let you read it the first time. Charlotte suffered delusions and wrote about them. I don't want your own thinking to be influenced by those delusions."

Don't try arguing with a psychologist. It's impossible.

I took my wallet, which had thirty dollars left from the birthday money Grandma had sent me, and shoved it into the pocket of my cutoffs. Jolie and I hiked two blocks to the bus stop.

We'd been to the Quarter often enough to know how to get there. Every time visitors come to New Orleans they have to see the French Quarter, so people who live in a suburb, like Metairie, are always taking relatives and friends to the

53

Quarter. Sometimes, too, on special occasions Mom, Dad, and I visit the Quarter just to enjoy one of the really great restaurants.

Jolie and I left Canal Street and walked into the Quarter's nearest cross street. Sure enough, just four blocks in was a small, tacky-looking shop with a dusty window displaying all sorts of candles and jars of dark powder, and even a bone.

Jolie looked at the faded nameplate over the door and translated from the French. "It's named Good Luck," she said. "It doesn't say anything about voodoo."

"Just look in the window," I told her. "They've got to sell charms and stuff."

We walked up a flight of three steps, opened a door, and entered the most cluttered room I'd ever seen in my life. The walls were covered with shelves, and on the shelves was an array of boxes, jars, and bottles. A woman, twice as wide as the door we'd just come through, sat behind a chipped and stained wooden counter.

"Whatcha want?" she asked in a high, singsong voice. She shoved a strand of greasy brown hair out of her puffy eyes and looked us up and down.

I wished I could turn and run. But I couldn't. I had to get the help I needed before I visited Graymoss. I cleared my throat a couple of times, wishing that Jolie would stop cringing behind me, and managed to speak. "I'm going to visit a house that has something evil in it," I said. "I need protection from the evil."

The woman nodded. "That's okay then. I'd get in trouble with the law if I sold you bad voodoo. Good voodoo is okay. Protection is okay."

"You mean you can do it?" Eagerly I took a step closer to the counter.

Jolie stepped out from behind me. "You can really protect her so she won't get hurt?"

"Sure. I'll mix up a bag of gris-gris. You wear it on a string around your neck. Tuck it inside your blouse. It'll keep the ghosts away from you."

"And get rid of them?" Jolie asked.

Shaking her head, the woman said, "No, no, no. I didn't say that. Getting rid of ghosts is something else altogether. Some people burn brimstone, but that doesn't work for me. First you gotta know why the ghost is there and second you gotta understand the ghost's problem so you can help it to free itself. And then you say, 'Go away to whatever awaits you,' to the ghost. Gris-gris can't do that. But it can keep ghosts from bothering you."

Jolie tugged on my arm. "That's what you want, isn't it? Protection while you're there. Your parents won't want to stay, so you'll come home, and that will be the end of it."

"Yes," I said. "That is what I want."

The woman mixed up all kinds of powders and tied them up in a very small cloth bag, about the size of a Ping-Pong ball, only flatter. She tied it tightly with a string and made a loop with the string so that I could wear it around my neck.

"What's in it?" I asked.

"You don't need to know," she said. "You just have to believe that it will protect you. And you can believe because I said that it will. Five dollars. You want to wear it now?"

"No," I said, giving her the money. "I don't need it yet. Could you put it in a paper bag?"

She reached under the counter and brought forth a small paper bag, used and wrinkled. She dropped the gris-gris charm into it.

I took it and thanked her, and Jolie and I left the store.

"Whew!" Jolie said when we were on the street with the door closed behind us. "I'm glad to be out of there."

I held the bag gingerly. "I'm the one who's got to wear the gris-gris," I said. "It looks weird. It even smells a little funny. What if it's got dead stuff in it or ground-up bones?"

Jolie stopped and faced me. "Don't back off now, Lia," she said. "Promise me that you'll wear it. Promise, or I won't be able to sleep or eat or do anything except worry until you come home. Promise!"

"All right," I said reluctantly. "I promise."


In Louisiana in the summertime the sun rises early and hot, so even though my alarm clock was on roll-over-and-go-back-to-sleep time, Dad knocked at my door and called, "Wake up, Lia. We want to get an early start."

I staggered out of bed, groaning, but as my mind began to wake up I remembered we were going to Graymoss. I hurried to dress and gulp down my breakfast. Not knowing what else to do with my gris-gris bag, I wore it, hidden inside the neck of my blue chambray shirt.

We drove Highway 61 to 190, a little north of Baton Rouge, where we turned east until we reached Highway 1. Then we drove north, following the Mississippi River.

Mom used the cell phone to make a couple of calls to the engineers. Finally I heard her say, "Not until Friday morning? That's the earliest you can make it? . . . Yes. Fine. Nine o'clock. We'll be there when you arrive."

Dad laughed. "You didn't expect them to drop everything and come today, did you?"

"I guess I'm impatient," Mom said. "I just can't wait to find out the results of their inspection."

"Take it easy," Dad said. "We haven't even seen Graymoss yet."

The drive didn't take long, even though we stopped to ask directions in a small town called Bogue City, which Mom said was close to Graymoss.

"Bogue City? Someone had dreams of grandeur," Dad said. He glanced down the main street and chuckled.

"Derek! Hush!" Mom said. She had already rolled down the window to talk to a portly, balding man who was strolling down the sidewalk.

"Sir," she called, "we're looking for a plantation house called Graymoss. Do you know of it? Can you tell us how to find it?"

The man stepped over to the car and bent down, peering through the open window at the three of us. He seemed satisfied at what he saw and stuck his arm through the window to shake hands. "The name's Walter Mudd," he said.

"Glad to meet you," Dad told him, and introduced himself, Mom, and me.

"So you're looking for Graymoss," Mr. Mudd said. "Well, you came to the right place. Everybody around here knows of Graymoss. But nobody's asked about the place for a long time. You don't look like the kind of folks that used to come."

Dad enjoyed interesting situations, and he liked to strike up conversations with people. His philosophy was that each person was different. Each one had something new to talk about. I didn't always agree with Dad. He was nice to everyone and he was usually upbeat. People liked him.

"What kind of folks were they?" Dad asked Mr. Mudd.

"Couple of ghost hunters came—at least that's what they called themselves," Mr. Mudd said. "Then a few years later somebody wrote about Graymoss for one of the state magazines. And five years ago Hannah Lord—she's president of the Bogue City Historical Society, has been for years—anyhow, Hannah wrote to some TV producer about Graymoss being haunted and how it would make a good TV show."

"So the producer came?"

"No. Nobody came. He didn't even answer Hannah's letter."

Mom smiled. "How do we get to Graymoss from here?"

Mr. Mudd studied Mom. "Are you just curious about the place, or do you have business there?"

"I'm the new owner," Mom said.

Mr. Mudd's eyes widened with excitement. He gave a little hop and glanced across the street where an old-fashioned red-and-white barber pole stood in front of a barber shop. It was easy to see that he could hardly wait to hurry to the barber shop and begin spreading the news.

"You take this road about one mile to a cutoff," he told us, "and turn to the right. About another mile further you'll see a gate—it won't be locked—and a drive. The house is at the end of the drive."

"I understand there's a caretaker. Will he be there?"

"Old Charlie Boudreau? Oh, sure. Charlie takes his job seriously. He'll be on hand."

"Thank you, Mr. Mudd," Mom said. "I guess we'll soon be neighbors."

Mr. Mudd started. "Neighbors? You don't mean you're thinking of living there?"

"That's exactly what I do mean," Mom answered.

"But . . . you must have heard about the haunts and the murders."

I eagerly leaned forward. "Murders? What murders?"

"I don't have all the details," Mr. Mudd said. "But over the years I've heard plenty of stories about folks seeking shelter in the dead of night and found the next morning dead of fright."

"They're stories. That's all they are—stories," Mom said. "We have great plans for Graymoss."

"Like what?" Mr. Mudd actually licked his lips in his eagerness to be first with the news.

Dad spoke up. "Before we make any definite plans, we'll have the house thoroughly checked by engineers for structural defects."

"They won't find much wrong, if anything," Mr.

59

Mudd replied. "Those old plantation houses were built to last, if they were properly cared for. Cedar and brick. The columns are brick plastered over. Good hardwood floors on the insides. No problems with termites. Needs paint here and there, but . . ." He stopped and then added, "But there's no way you can live there. Not with the goings-on in the house."

Mom opened her mouth as if she were going to argue, but she apparently thought better of it because she said, "We'll see, Mr. Mudd. Thank you for your help."

Mr. Mudd stepped back, Mom rolled up the window, and Dad drove on down the road. I twisted around to look back, and there was Mr. Mudd trotting as fast as he could go across the street toward the barber shop.

Dad followed the directions Mr. Mudd had given us, and in just a few minutes we turned into the drive that led to Graymoss. Beyond an ornate wrought iron gate the drive was lined with huge oak trees, their branches dripping with long fingers of the gray moss that seems to feed on the trees. There weren't as many oaks as at the famous plantation Oak Alley, and the rows weren't as long, but the house that stood at the end of the drive was stately and gleaming white in the sunlight.

"Oh, Derek!" Mom cried. "It's wonderful! It's picture-perfect!"

The house was a tall two stories. Verandas, supported by rows of tall columns, wrapped around both the lower and the upper story. Steps from the curving drive led to the center of the lower veranda. Beyond, deep in shadow, was a massive wooden front door. On either side and on the second story, sheer curtains hung at windows that were also shaded by the wide verandas. There were patches here and there where brick showed through worn spots on the columns.

"A little plaster, a new coat of paint," Dad said. He sounded excited.

"Oh, Derek!" Mom cried again. "I'll open the gate. I can't wait to see all of the house!"

I patted the spot where the bag of gris-gris lay under my shirt. Under my trembling fingers I could feel the pounding of my heart. Whatever made me think that I could face the evil that haunted Graymoss?

# CHAPTER SIX

From around a corner of the house came a tall, lean man in overalls. Wisps of white hair stuck out from under his broad-brimmed straw hat. I guess he had heard our car. As he stood next to his pickup, he looked at us with curiosity.

"Are y'all lost?" he called.

Mom hopped from the car. "No," she said, and walked toward him. Dad and I joined her, and she introduced us. "You must be Mr. Charles Boudreau," she added.

He nodded. "Folks around here just call me Charlie. You can call me Charlie, too. That's what I'm used to answerin' to. I'm the caretaker here."

Mom smiled like a little kid at Christmas. "I'm the new owner of Graymoss, Charlie."

"What happened to Mrs. Langley?"

"Mrs. Langley was my grandmother. She died and left Graymoss to me," Mom explained.

Charlie removed his hat, leaving a damp halo where his hair stuck tightly to his sweaty scalp. "I'm mighty sorry to hear she passed on," he said. "I only met Mrs. Langley once, but she sent checks regular, right on the dot."

"I'll keep the checks coming," Mom said. "Even after we move into Graymoss, we'll still need your help."

"Move in?" Charlie stared in surprise. "You surely ain't plannin' to live in the house, are you?"

Dad spoke up. "Why not? It seems to be in fair condition. It shouldn't be too hard to make it livable."

He turned to get a closer look at the house. The deep veranda, dim and cool in the morning's heat, beckoned invitingly. I suppose Dad felt it, too. All the veranda needed was a porch swing and a table that would hold lemonade glasses and a stack of good books.

Turning back to Charlie, Dad asked, "Are you concerned about repairs that might be needed on the house?"

Charlie clapped his hat back on his head. "Some repairs are probable, but I'm not talkin' about repairs alone. The inside kitchen's impossible. You wouldn't want to try cookin' in it. There's no gas in the house, and no electricity, and no indoor plumbin'. There's a four-hole privy out back—at least what remains of it. I wouldn't try to use it, if I was you."

"Yuck!" I blurted out. "No real bathrooms? We can't stay here tonight!"

Mom looked surprised. "We have no plans to spend the night. We'll be driving back to Metairie."

"If the structure's sound, indoor plumbing can be added," Dad said to Charlie. "Also electricity."

Charlie slowly shook his head as if he couldn't believe what he was hearing. "I don't think y'all are gonna want to do that on account of nobody can set foot in the house after it starts turnin' dark."

Mom sighed. "I suppose you're referring to those silly stories about haunts roaming through the rooms."

"You're the first person I've met who called the haunts silly," he answered. "Most people don't see anythin' funny about gettin' scared out of their wits, especially those folks who got themselves frightened to death."

"Tell us about the murders," Dad said. "You've been working here a long time, so you must have been the one who found the bodies."

"Not me," Charlie said. "None of that stuff happened since I started working here back in sixty-nine. If I'd come across a dead body, I wouldn't be here now."

"So these were just stories you'd heard," Dad said.

Charlie shrugged. "Everybody knows about 'em."

"I don't believe anyone died of fright in this house, because I know that ghosts don't exist," Mom told him firmly. "Whatever local stories and legends have built up about Graymoss are simply imaginative hysteria."

"Yes, ma'am," Charlie said. "Except that the stories about the evil are for real, all right. Stay until after dark and you'll see for yourself. Just don't ask me to stick around."

Mom impatiently looked at her watch. "I'd like to take a look at the interior of the house, Charlie. Do you have a key?"

"I sure do," he said, and pulled a ring of keys from the back pocket of his overalls. He held it out to Mom, pointing at two of the keys. "Front door and back door. I woulda got May—that's my wife—to come to dust and sweep if I'd known you was goin' to visit. She cleans once a month or so just to keep things in order. The cleanin's not too regular since people don't live here."

Mom began walking toward the veranda. "I'd like to meet May. I'd be happy if she'd continue her help with the house, too. Do you think she'd be agreeable?"

"Oh, May's almost always agreeable," Charlie said. "It's just that she don't like bein' in the house, and she'd never stay past late afternoon." He shrugged as Mom, Dad, and I began to climb the steps to the veranda. "It won't matter anyhow, because if you stay here till it grows dark, you'll change your plans in a hurry."

Before Dad opened the massive front door, he turned to look at Charlie. "Do you want to come with us? Show us around?"

"No, thanks," Charlie answered. "You ought to be able to figure out where you are and where you're goin' pretty well by yourselves. I've got to finish the work I started in the vegetable garden."

"Oh! You've kept up the garden?" Mom did that happy clapping hands thing again. I winced.

"May and me have been growin' our own vegetables here for quite some years," he said. "I hope that's all right with you."

"Of course," Mom said. "I'm counting on a big vegetable garden—one that will feed a very large family." She glanced at Dad and giggled.

"Oh," Charlie said. "You've got more'n one kid."

"We will have," Mom said, and giggled again.

I was totally embarrassed. I wanted to tell Charlie, "It isn't what you think. She's talking about adopting children." But then I thought, *Why should I worry about what Charlie thinks? We won't be here anyway. No adopted kids. No living in this haunted house. So why bother?*

Charlie might have been puzzled, but he didn't ask any more questions. "When y'all are through with seein' the house, you can bring me back the keys," he said. "I'll show you the outbuildings. There's the barn, which you probably noticed, and a root cellar, and the summer kitchen. All part of the property, except that the summer kitchen's about to fall down. No fault of mine. It just wasn't built to last, like the house was."

"What's a summer kitchen?" I asked.

Dad answered my question. "Cooking inside the house added a great deal of heat in the summer, so cooking used to be done outside in an outbuilding."

Mom was having trouble hiding her excitement. I knew how badly she wanted to see the house. "Thank you, Charlie," she said, and turned to Dad. "Please open the door, Derek. Hurry!"

The massive door swung open on dry hinges with a whining, grinding noise. It startled me so that I jumped back and grabbed the railing that edged the veranda.

"Been meanin' to oil those hinges," Charlie called. "I'll do that tomorrow."

I took a deep breath, rested my hand on the bag of gris-gris under my shirt, then followed Mom and Dad into the house.

The entry hall was spacious, with a curving stairway that swept up the right side of the hall to a second-floor landing.

"Oh, it's beautiful, Derek!" Mom cried.

"Some of the paint on the paneling is peeling," I said. "And look over there. The wallpaper is curling up."

"That doesn't matter. Paint and wallpaper are easy to replace," Mom said. "Come this way. There seems to be a dining room on this side."

I lagged behind as Mom and Dad hurried into the dining room. I tried to imagine the scary things that had happened to people in this house, but with sunlight streaming through the windows it was hard to believe they had actually taken place. I began to wonder if Mom was right and the stories were imagination or hysteria or whatever else a psychologist would call them.

The dining room was immense, with a long mahogany table that had room for lots of extra leaves. Mom hugged Dad and squealed, "It's big enough for a very large family! How perfect can it get!"

An ornate, very dusty crystal chandelier hung over the table, and I leaned back to stare up at it. I couldn't begin to count all the candle stubs that were still in their tarnished silver holders. How many, many years had it been since their light glowed throughout this room? Radiating outward from the spot where the chandelier was attached to the ceiling were ornate plaster vines and leaves and flowers. They spread across the ceiling to each corner, where they met the same kind of design that outlined the borders between the ceiling and the four walls.

Mom and Dad took one look at me and stared upward, too.

"That gorgeous chandelier must be the original one. I can't believe it wasn't stolen out of the house," Mom said. She slowly turned around. "Or this beautiful highboy, or the rest of the furniture. Over all these years weren't there thieves or vandals in this area?"

"The evil in the house kept them away," I explained.

Mom gave me one of those looks, so I quickly added, "You read the diary. Charlotte wrote that no one dared to come near the house."

"I don't want to hear another word about ghosts!" Mom practically exploded.

But Dad smiled and put an arm around her shoulders. "Instead of feeling impatient about the house's ghostly reputation, you can be thankful that everyone was afraid of it," he said. "It looks as though the spooky stories kept people away. The house has waited all these years just for us."

A cold chill shivered up and down my backbone. What Dad had said made me think of Sarah's words: "Graymoss is there. It's waiting." I didn't want whatever was in this house to wait for us. I fingered the bag of gris-gris again. Just knowing it was there and I was protected made me feel a whole lot better.

At least Mom's good humor had been restored. I trailed along behind her and Dad as they walked through the kitchen, a storage room Mom called a butler's pantry, some other rooms that had probably been parlors, and into a library.

The library had been cut off from the full brightness of the sunlight by ancient, deep blue velvet drapes pulled partly closed. The drapes were not only badly faded, they were tattered, almost shredded in places as though cat claws had ripped through them. I didn't touch them. I was afraid they'd disintegrate on the spot.

The shelves that lined one of the walls all the way to the ceiling were mostly filled with books, but the leather and cloth bindings on many of them had rotted, and their yellowed pages had curled. I tried to read the titles and authors on the spines of the books that were still intact, but the gold lettering was so tarnished on some of them it was impossible to make out any words. On the books that were in better condition I didn't recognize the names of the books or the authors.

"I wish I could take all these books with me," I said, but Mom and Dad weren't there to answer me. I could hear their footsteps on the stairs. I wondered if Charlotte had read all these books. If I'd been Charlotte, I would have. If I lived here now . . .

I glanced around the room again, holding tightly to my bag of gris-gris. "I suppose you can't hear me, whoever you are," I said to the ghost that haunted Graymoss, "since you've only been known to come out after dark. But in case you're kind of hanging back, listening, I want you to know something. No matter what Mom and Dad keep talking about, we're not going to live here. They want to fill this house with kids. Think about it. Kids yelling and fighting and running up and down stairs and shouting at the tops of their lungs . . ."

I added, "I don't want it. You don't want it. We've got that much in common. Okay? So if I can keep Mom here after dark, just go ahead and do your scariest thing and make her want to leave. If you're as terrifying as Charlotte wrote that you were, then Mom will be just like all the other Women Who Are Exceptionally Brave in our family and cop out."

The room was silent. Mom's and Dad's voices faded in and out from a great distance as they explored the upstairs bedrooms.

No one answered me, but I wasn't expecting an answer. I'd come to terms with whatever was in this house, and I felt a lot more relaxed. I let go of the gris-gris and reached on tiptoe for a volume that had once been bound in dark red leather. What was left of the title made me think it contained stories of King Arthur and his Round Table of knights.

I managed to get a grip on the book and gave a tug. It didn't budge, but suddenly, from out of nowhere, a thin book fell, zooming past my head and whacking me on the shoulder.

"Ouch!" I said. I let go of the book I'd been trying for and rubbed my shoulder.

Cautiously I glanced around the dimly lit room. No one had entered it. I was alone. It was foolish to think that ghosts had dropped this book on me. It was daylight, not dark. There were no stories that recorded strange goings-on in Graymoss in broad daylight, so it couldn't have been a ghost. Somehow, in trying to pull down one book, I'd accidentally dislodged another. It was as simple as that.

I tried to make myself believe it.

Bending down, I picked up the book, took a good look at it, and nearly dropped it again. The cover was a soft leather, stained, with one corner singed. It seemed impossible, after all these years, but the book smelled faintly of smoke. I was positive that in my hands was the book Charlotte's grandfather had given to her—the one with the answers to her questions. It was the book that Cousin Lydia had taken away from Charlotte and hidden. The title gleamed up at me: *Favorite Tales of Edgar Allan Poe*.

My knees began to wobble, and for a moment I had trouble breathing. I backed up and landed in a wing-backed chair, sending up a puff of dust. It wasn't an accident that I'd been hit by this book. Somebody—or something—wanted me to have it.

"Why me?" I asked aloud. I'd read some of Edgar Allan Poe's stories in American lit—"The

71

Murders in the Rue Morgue," "The Gold Bug," and "The Cask of Amontillado," and they were creepy because such awful things happened to the characters in the stories. Somebody throttled and stuffed up a chimney, somebody's skull nailed to a tree, and somebody walled up inside a wine cellar and left to die.

No one answered my spoken question. But the memory of what Charlotte had written in her diary jumped into my mind. "The answers to your questions are in these pages," her grandfather had told her. I well remembered.

Another thought struck me. Supposing I'd been given this book for a reason, and the reason was that I should find the answers that Charlotte hadn't been able to find. What answers? The Civil War was long over. Morgan Slade had disappeared with the Blevins family treasures. I examined the book carefully. Both endpapers had peeled back from the binding enough to show me there had been no secret notes pasted inside. There was nothing in the book that would tell me where Slade had gone or what had happened to the Blevinses' treasures.

"Why give this book to me?" I asked aloud. "I don't think you just want me to read it, so what am I supposed to do with it?"

A breeze broke the stale air in the room, ruffling the hair that hung around my face. Closing my eyes, I enjoyed the coolness and the soft fragrance of cut grass and summer sun.

But my eyelids flew open, and I gasped as I realized that I couldn't have felt a breeze—at least not a real one. All the windows in the dimly lit room were tightly closed, with the drapes partly drawn across them.

I clutched *Favorite Tales of Edgar Allan Poe* to my chest and ran out of the library. I'd asked a question of my own, and something had given me its answer.

# CHAPTER SEVEN

I raced upstairs and found Mom and Dad standing in one of the bedrooms. Mom was holding a measuring tape, intent on the width of the windows, so neither of them paid any attention to my sudden appearance. I leaned against the wall for support while I caught my breath.

The furniture was heavy and massive, with thick, carved spindles holding up what was left of the canopy over the tester bed. The sheer, once-white fabric must have covered the canopy and hung down the sides to protect the sleeper from mosquitoes, but now it hung from the framework in long, stringy tatters. It made me think of the horrible, gray strings of moss that hung from the oaks outside the house. Deep upholstered chairs flanked the fireplace with its black marble mantel, and in one corner sat a large cat cut out of polished black stone.

Mom was saying, "Since this is the largest bedroom—"

I interrupted. "If this was the largest bedroom, then wouldn't it have belonged to Placide Blevins, Charlotte's grandfather?"

"It might have," Dad answered. "The furniture looks like something a man would find comfortable."

I glanced again at the bed. A muted green-and-gold brocade spread covered the mattress and the pillows; sheets and blankets, I guessed, were underneath. This must have been where the workers had brought the body of Charlotte's grandfather. She had washed and dressed his body here, and she had sat with him until the horror in the house had frightened her away.

I looked up at the ceiling, half closing my eyes as Charlotte had. The flowers and leaves and ornate scrolls turned to small faces, and for just a moment I could feel their eyes staring back at me.

Shivering, I forced my glance away and wrapped my arms around myself. *Mr. Blevins,* I thought, *you aren't the terrifying evil in this house. You loved Charlotte. You would never have done anything to frighten her.* But I wondered about the evil. It hadn't been in the house before the grandfather's death. So where had it come from? Why was it here? What did it want?

Mom and Dad walked into the hallway. "I like the idea of two children to a room instead of a dormitory plan," Mom said to Dad. "That means we won't have to remove any walls. But if we eventually adopt more than a dozen—"

She began talking about bunk beds, but I stopped hearing her because before my eyes the center of the mattress seemed to sink. I could see the indentation a body would make if someone had been lying on his back, right in the middle of the bed.

Someone *was* lying on the bed! Someone I couldn't see!

I tried to move, but couldn't. I seemed to be stuck to the floor. But my mouth must have opened because Mom and Dad ran into the room.

"Lia! Why are you screaming?" Mom cried out.

With my left hand I grabbed my bag of gris-gris, wadding up a fistful of shirt. I didn't let go of the book I held in my right hand as I pointed to the bed. "Look! You can see the depression in the middle of the bed! Someone's lying on it!"

"Who?"

"I don't know!" I shouted. "He's invisible!"

Mom's voice was soft and controlled. "Lia, dear, there's no depression on the bed," she said.

I blinked and looked again. She was right. The bed looked just as it had when I first entered the room.

Dad put an arm around my shoulders and gave me a playful squeeze. He picked up my right hand, turning it so that he could read the title of the book. "Edgar Allan Poe? Lia, my little book lover, you're letting your imagination run away with you. You're reading too many ghost stories."

Mom said, "I never should have let you read that awful diary."

I leaned against Dad, my knees wobbly. "It doesn't matter what I read. A body *was* lying there," I told them. "It wasn't my imagination. I saw it."

"You just think you did," Dad said.

"I *know* I did."

"Your imagination can play tricks with your mind," he told me. "Under the right circumstances it can make you think you see things you don't."

Mom looked at me strangely. "Why are you clutching the neck of your shirt like that?" she asked. "It's going to be full of wrinkles."

As I looked down at my hand I realized what had happened to change things. It was the gris-gris. When I had it under my hand everything was normal. But when I let go of it . . . I had let go to reach for the book, and that was when *Favorite Tales of Edgar Allan Poe* had been dropped on me. I wasn't holding the gris-gris when I saw the indentation on the bed, but when I grabbed it the indentation went away.

"You didn't answer my question," Mom said.

I wasn't about to. Just try telling Mom and Dad about gris-gris!

I flattened my hand and tried to smooth out my shirt, careful to keep the bag under my fingers. "Sorry," I said. "I got excited."

Dad looked at his watch. As he spoke to Mom, he gave me a quick glance, which I wasn't supposed to see, and said, "I think we've spent enough time in the house for now. We can't make definite plans until we've received the engineers' report. Let's find Mr. Boudreau and take a quick look at the outbuildings. Then we'll go back to Baton Rouge and have lunch."

"And come back to Graymoss this evening," I said. I'd invited the evil in the house to do its best with Mom. She and Dad had to drop their plans before they went too far. I wasn't going to like whatever would happen, but it had to be. Mom and Dad had to be convinced that we couldn't live at Graymoss.

Mom shook her head and said, "We're not going to come back here this evening, Lia. Those stories in the diary have you frightened even in the daylight. Just think what your imagination might do to you after dark."

"But . . ." I didn't know what to say. I couldn't tell her why it was important to me that she and Dad see and hear and feel the full fury of the evil. I blurted out, "Don't you want to prove to me the stories are just that . . . stories? Make-believe?"

"No, Lia. Not today."

"Really, Mom, I want to come back. I—"

"Don't argue. It won't do any good," Mom said. She put a hand on Dad's shoulder. "Let's do as your father suggested. We'll lock up the house and find Mr. Boudreau."

Mom and Dad walked down the stairs to the entry hall. All I could do was follow and try to come up with an idea about what to do next.

"Mr. and Mrs. Starling?"

A deep voice from behind us boomed out so suddenly, I jumped and let out a yelp. I wasn't alone. Mom started, and Dad whirled around to face whoever was there.

Out of the dining room strode a tall, broad-shouldered man who was dressed in a suit and tie in spite of the day's heat. His nose was long and so thin that it made me think of a fence dividing his close-set eyes. His hair was thick and the kind of shiny black that comes from a bottle of dye. He smiled and held out a hand to Dad. "The name's Raymond Merle, and you must be the Starlings. Glad to meet you," he said, without giving Mom or Dad a chance to say a word.

All I got was a brisk nod as he handed Dad a business card and went on talking. He had to be one of those people who think kids don't exist. It didn't bother me. I was used to adults who acted like that.

"I'm a land developer," he explained. "I represent a firm that has big plans for Bogue City."

Dad's mouth twitched, and I could tell he wanted to laugh. "Bogue City's a pretty small place. What kind of plans could be called *big* plans?"

Mr. Merle's eyes narrowed even more. "The size of Bogue City doesn't matter, although Main Street will be spruced up, a few stores will be added, and maybe a movie theater. What we're talking about is right here, on this riverfront property—a self-contained retirement community."

"Not here," Mom managed to squeeze in, but Mr. Merle went right on as though he hadn't heard her.

"We're talking about cottages with kitchenettes and river views for those who want more independence," he said. "Then, behind the cottages, a four-story building with luxury apartments, restaurant, coffee shop, and entertainment center.

There'll be a medical center with a nurse on the premises, and a doctor just a quick call away. On the east side of the property we'll build a golf course and small clubhouse. On the west, a row of shops—groceries, clothing, gifts. Walking trails, biking trails—you name it, we'll have it."

"No," Mom said.

Mr. Merle stared at the high ceiling and waved his arms in a wide arc. "All this should have been torn down years ago," he said. "I shudder when I think of all the money spent on taxes and upkeep. As the new owner, I know you'll be tickled to get the place off your hands."

Mom tried again. "Listen to me."

But Mr. Merle was like a windup toy that hadn't reached the end of its spring. "I'd like to sit down with you in my office and come to an understanding. I can offer you a mighty fine price for this property."

Mom leaned toward Mr. Merle, tilting her face up so that she was almost nose to nose with him. "You haven't heard me, Mr. Merle," she said. "This property is not for sale to you, to the firm you're working with, or to anyone else. It's mine, and my husband and I have our own plans for it."

Mr. Merle's glance grew even sharper as he studied Mom's face. He looked as if he were trying to read her mind. "You plan to develop the property?" he asked.

"We plan to develop it the way it should be developed. We intend to turn Graymoss into a family home for a group of children."

Mr. Merle actually snickered. "You haven't

heard the stories about what goes on in this house after dark."

"I've heard the stories, and I've read Charlotte Blevins's diary," Mom said.

"Then you know that Charlotte wasn't the only one who felt the haunts," he said.

Mom's voice became cool and detached as she said, "There is clinical terminology for the type of mass hysteria that has been engendered by the legends surrounding Graymoss."

Mr. Merle backed off. He studied Mom with those sharp little eyes of his and said, "That's what you think it is—mass hysteria? How wrong can you be?"

Mom drew herself up. "I am not wrong, Mr. Merle. I'm a psychologist. Throughout the years, I have worked with people who are disturbed. I know how fear can grow, how people can actually cling to it."

For a moment Mr. Merle was silent. Then he said, "All I can say is, spend one night in this house, Mrs. Starling, and you'll change your mind real quick."

I gripped the bag of gris-gris and Poe's book with all my might, holding my breath as I waited for Mom's answer. I was rooting for Mr. Merle to win this one. *Dare her!* I thought, hoping he'd pick up the mental message. *Make her take the dare!*

Mom smiled, but it wasn't a friendly smile. "If I do, I suppose you'll provide clanking chains and sheeted 'ghosts' who moan and groan—all the correct ghostly effects."

Mr. Merle's face flushed a dark red. "I don't use tactics like that to make a sale," he said.

"I apologize," Mom said, although she didn't look the least bit sorry. "I just want to make it perfectly clear to you and to everyone else that I have no intention of selling this house and property. My husband and I have dreams of turning it into a home for unadoptable children—children who have very little chance of growing up with parents who love them and care for them."

"I've always heard there aren't enough babies to adopt," Mr. Merle countered.

For the first time Dad stepped into the conversation. He'd been hanging back, leaning against the round table in the center of the entry hall. He'd let Mom carry the ball herself, the smile in his eyes showing that he knew she'd come out the winner. "You're right about the babies," he said. "Most people wanting to adopt do want babies. They aren't interested in older children—especially two or three in a family who want to stick together. And they usually don't want children who are mentally or physically handicapped." Dad's smile broadened as he added, "But we do."

For a moment I felt smothered by a heavy wave of guilt, but I pushed it away. Mom and Dad weren't the only ones in this family. I was here, too. Sure, I felt sorry for kids who needed homes, but I wasn't ready for a dozen instant brothers and sisters. And I didn't like the idea of living way off from nowhere with Bogue City as the only nearby town. Graymoss was too far from Jolie. We'd never be able to get together. I was getting desperate.

Before Mom or Dad could say anything more about filling this house with kids, I broke in. "Let's come back tonight, Mom," I said. "We'll prove that there's nothing scary about this house and that Mr. Merle is wrong."

Mom raised an eyebrow as she looked at me. "Not tonight," she said firmly.

"Don't worry about *me*," I began, but Dad interrupted.

"You're our beloved daughter, and we *do* worry about you." He grinned as he said, "We'll make sure we banish all the ghosts and goblins from our minds, then move on to the next step."

"And come here at night?"

"You better come soon," Mr. Merle said, "before you start pouring money into this place."

*Good move*, I thought, sending Mr. Merle more mental messages. *Keep it up. Say something that will make Mom want to be here after dark.*

But Mom didn't give him a chance. She opened the front door and said impatiently, "Mr. Merle, there'll be no more talk about ghosts. We've been in this house close to two hours, and we haven't seen a single sign of preternatural beings."

He shrugged. "That's because it's daylight. The ghostly stuff waits until after dark."

"Only after dark? But—" I blurted out, then stopped as the three of them looked at me.

At least one ghost hadn't waited. I'd only been in Graymoss a few minutes when it had let me know of its presence. In spite of the sun-baked air pouring through the open door, I grew cold and shivered. All these years . . . all this time . . . had the ghost been waiting for *me*?

83

# CHAPTER EIGHT

I was counting on the promise that nothing invisible could harm me as long as I held on to the gris-gris, but I was still the first one out the door. As I walked across the veranda and down the steps, I was puzzled by what had happened and why.

Mom and Dad said a quick goodbye to Mr. Merle. He folded himself into a low black sports car and drove off, obviously unhappy about the way things had turned out.

"I never want to see that awful man again," Mom declared.

"You won't get your wish," Dad said. "He'll be back to follow through. You didn't even let him make his offer."

Mom shook her head impatiently. "How could

he actually think that a few ridiculous ghost stories would send us running?"

"Because the other women in the family ran," I said.

Mom's nose and cheeks got pink, the way they always did when she was upset, so I spoke fast. "There was something in the house that frightened them. That's what Grandma said. But the house doesn't frighten you, Mom. At least it doesn't right now."

"What do you mean by that?" Mom asked.

"I mean, prove that everyone else is wrong. Stay in the house at night." I threw in something I thought would really make my case. "Don't let Mr. Merle win," I told her.

"Mr. Merle is *not* going to win," Mom snapped. She hadn't said that we wouldn't come back after dark, so I began to hope.

Mom turned to Dad. "How did he find out so quickly that we were here?"

"You know small towns," Dad answered. "News travels fast."

"Especially when the newscaster is someone like Mr. Mudd," I said.

Dad and I laughed. Mom was getting over being angry, because at least she smiled.

"I want to see the outbuildings," Dad said.

"And the vegetable garden," Mom said.

We had no sooner walked across the drive and onto the thick, green lawn when we heard a car driving up. We stopped and stared as a gold Cadillac zoomed up the drive and stopped with a screech next to our own car.

A plump woman, with piled-up hair bleached the bright yellow of lemons, heaved herself out of the passenger seat of the car. "Yoo-hoo!" she called.

I lost interest in her as I noticed the hunk climbing out of the driver's side. He was tall and good-looking, with dark hair and blue eyes. I guessed he was around sixteen or seventeen. The woman made straight for Mom and Dad, but the guy smiled, his eyes on mine.

"Good morning, good morning," the woman called. "You have got to be the Starlings, the new owners of Graymoss, and I'm delighted to meet you. I'm Hannah Lord. This is my grandson, Jonathan."

We all said hello and went through introductions.

"Hi, Lia," Jonathan said in a voice that was warm and deep.

I had to gulp before I could answer. My "Hi" came out in a squeak.

"Let's step inside out of the sun," Mom said. "I'm sorry that I can't offer you anything to eat or drink."

Mrs. Lord giggled and said, "Thank you. I didn't expect refreshments." She took Mom's arm and leaned into her ear. "I must confess that I've been dying to see the interior of Graymoss. Mr. Boudreau takes his caretaker duties seriously. He won't allow anyone inside—even for a tiny peek."

We all walked back up the stairs, and Dad unlocked the front door again.

Mrs. Lord clasped a hand to her chest and took

a loud breath. "Oh, my! I can't tell you how excited I am!" she cried.

She gasped her way around the entry hall and through the downstairs rooms. As we silently followed behind her, I made sure the bag of gris-gris stayed right under the fingers of my left hand.

"It's perfect! This house is absolutely perfect!" Mrs. Lord cried as we reached the parlor. She dropped onto a nearby sofa and fanned herself with her small handbag.

"Thank you. We think so, too," Mom said.

Mrs. Lord leaned forward, her eyes bright. "I modestly neglected to tell you that I'm president of the Bogue City Historical Society. I've been president for eons because no one else could match my devotion and dedication to the position."

"Or want the job," Jonathan murmured into my ear. He was standing very close. Smiling, I turned to share the joke, and my cheek brushed his shoulder. I desperately wished I could think of something clever to say. I didn't know how to talk to guys. I didn't know how to talk to anybody but Jolie.

Mrs. Lord took a deep breath and went on. "Just think how fantastic it would be to share this piece of local history with those who'd drive from all over the country to see it!"

"I beg your pardon?" Mom said.

"On historical tours," Mrs. Lord said. "Tours to the old plantation homes are all the thing. They're even combined with some of the steamboat cruises on the Mississippi. But, of course, you know all that. You must, if you read the newspa-

pers. Think what exhibiting our own local planta-
tion would do for the economy of Bogue City!
And to the prestige of our Bogue City Historical
Society!"

She didn't say, "and to me," but the words were
hanging there.

Mom shook her head. "Are you asking me to
turn Graymoss over to your historical society?"

"That's exactly what I'm asking." Mrs. Lord
beamed at Mom. "Taxwise it could be highly ad-
vantageous to you."

"I'm not—" Mom began.

"Oh! I have such dreams! We could put a small
gift shop in the kitchen area. Of course, we'd have
to have a new water well dug and a rest rooms area
built out in back. And then—"

"Absolutely not," Mom interrupted. "We have
other plans for Graymoss."

Mrs. Lord turned pale and sank against the back
of the sofa. "It's Ray Merle, isn't it? He got to you
first."

Mom opened her mouth to answer, but Mrs.
Lord suddenly revived and struggled to her feet.
"We'll meet his price, even though it will be difficult. We'll hold fund-raisers. We'll do whatever
needs to be done to raise the money. We can't let
him bulldoze this valuable contribution to history."

"It's not Mr. Merle," Mom tried to explain.

"Mr. Tavey, then. Don't even listen to Mr.
Tavey! He's dying to get his hands on the furnishings. You know, Tavey's Antiques. But he must
not have them. The furniture belongs with the
house!"

"Please listen to me, Mrs. Lord," Mom said. Her voice sounded tired. I don't think she'd had any idea she'd spend her time at Graymoss arguing with people who wanted the property. "My husband and I plan to modernize the house and turn it into a home for at least a dozen unadoptable children."

"But that's impossible! You can't!" Mrs. Lord insisted. "For one thing, Graymoss is a priceless piece of history and should be treated as such. The house was built in 1831 and survived the War Between the States. Through your family's trust, Graymoss has been well cared for, and I can see that it needs relatively little in repair. I can give you a long list of very good reasons why Graymoss should be opened to visitors as a historical treasure."

Mom looked cynical. "I suppose the first reason on your list is that we can't live in this house because of some kind of after-dark hocus-pocus."

"You mean the ghosts," Mrs. Lord said. "Since you know about the ghosts, I don't have to tell you about them. I assure you that the stories about the fearsome evil that takes place in Graymoss after dark are not exaggerated."

Mom's eyebrow slid even higher. Cynically, she asked, "You don't think that the so-called ghosts will frighten visitors away?"

Mrs. Lord missed the sarcasm. "Oh, my dear, of course not," she said. "They'll be a fantastic selling point. The house won't be open at night, which is when the terrifying things take place. And people love tours through haunted houses. They love knowing that ghosts appear—only not in daylight hours. I know for a fact that when some of the plantation tours began including stories about the ghosts that haunt the premises, attendance rose dramatically."

I quickly asked, "The ghosts—uh—what about when they show up during the day?"

"They don't. At least not at Graymoss."

I had to persist, because I knew she was wrong. "Are you sure no one has seen any sign of ghosts in Graymoss during the day?"

"No one has ever reported any unusual occurrences," she said. "Believe me, as I told you, I've researched Graymoss thoroughly. Your mother," she told Mom in a voice filled with awe, "even allowed me to read Charlotte Blevins Porter's diary."

"This conversation is absurd," Mom said. "We're talking about ghosts as though they exist. Mrs. Lord, we don't believe in ghosts. We aren't going to be frightened away by tales of things that go bump in the night."

"But Charlotte's diary—" Mrs. Lord began.

"Charlotte was under a great deal of stress," Mom said. "She had recently been orphaned and lost her grandmother. She was terrified by the soldiers' threat to burn her house, and you can imagine how traumatized she was when her grandfather was shot right before her eyes. Hallucinating during tremendously stressful situations is not uncommon."

"It wasn't just Charlotte who experienced the evil," Mrs. Lord argued. "The workers Charlotte wrote about and her mother's cousin Lydia all saw, heard, and felt the same things as Charlotte."

"The results of the power of suggestion can be amazing," Mom told her.

"Oh, no, my dear," Mrs. Lord said. "I can't believe that the horrifying events Charlotte wrote about didn't exist. There have been people who have come to Graymoss just to experience manifestations. And there have been those whose intent was to steal or vandalize. The evil came. It terrified them. It drove them away. Some of them actually died of fright. In a sense you might say that the evil protected Graymoss."

Mom faced Mrs. Lord, eye-to-eye. "Can you give me the name of one single person who died of fright in this house?"

For just an instant Mrs. Lord stopped behaving like a commanding general. "In my research I was unable to find any documentation of the deaths. However—"

Mom wasn't about to give up. "Then can you tell me the names of those who have seen or heard this evil and are able to describe it to me?"

Mrs. Lord sucked in her breath, her chest heaving like an inflating balloon, and a smug smile spread across her lips. She looked at her grandson. "Tell her, Jonathan," she said. "Tell Mrs. Starling exactly what you went through."

# CHAPTER NINE

W e all turned to stare at Jonathan, who didn't seem to mind a bit. He even took a step forward. "I hope you understand I was just a kid when it happened," he said. "I was ten—almost eleven—and some of the guys started daring each other about who was brave enough to spend a night in the haunted house . . . uh, Graymoss, that is. And, well, you know how kids are."

Jonathan didn't begin his story by talking to all of us, as most people would. He directed what he said to Mom, as if she were the only one who needed to be convinced. For a few seconds I sort of wondered why, but I soon forgot everything else but Jonathan's story.

"Some of the guys came with me, but only as far as the gate. It was locked, so I climbed over and walked up the road to the house. Twice, strands of moss hung so low from the oak branches that they swept across my face, and I jumped and yelped.

"Luckily I had a flashlight, because it was awfully dark, with the moon mostly behind the clouds. The flashlight kept me from catching a foot in some of the ruts in the road."

Jonathan paused and grinned, ducking his head. "I was glad I had that light in any case, because I was really scared. I mean, there'd been a lot of talk about strange stuff going on around the house at night, and my friends weren't any help. They had a lot of fun scaring me before I left them to start up the road. As I came close to the house it loomed up like a monster. I stood just outside the veranda and almost stopped breathing as I stared into the windows for a long time. I just listened and waited."

Jonathan stopped talking for a moment, and I couldn't stand it. "What did you see in the house? Were there lights? Faces? What?"

"It doesn't matter, Lia," Mom said firmly. "I think we've heard enough of the story for now."

"Please let him finish," Mrs. Lord said. "Go ahead, Jonathan."

"Sure," Jonathan said, and glanced quickly at his grandmother. "It's just that when I think about it . . . well, sometimes I . . ." He looked back at Mom, took a deep breath, and continued. "I walked up on the veranda, slow and careful. I didn't want to make any more noise than I had to.

"I tried the front door, but it was locked. I knew it would be. So then I walked around to the back of the house and tried the kitchen door. It was locked, too. There were dark shapes around me that I couldn't figure out. I was really scared."

He cleared his throat. "I almost gave up and went home right then, but I saw that a window next to the kitchen door was open about an inch. I tried it and noticed that the lock was broken. I pushed it open and climbed through.

"I used my flashlight to make my way through the kitchen into some of the other rooms. I looked around for something comfortable. I mean, if I had to spend the night, I didn't want to be crammed into some hard chair. There was a big wing chair in a room with a lot of books in shelves along one side—"

"The library," I interrupted.

"I guess you could call it a library," Jonathan said. "I sat down and turned out my flashlight because I didn't think the batteries would last all night long. I knew I'd better save them in case of an emergency. The house was dark and quiet, and I started getting sleepy. Then all of a sudden a book came flying out of nowhere and hit my leg."

Jonathan's eyes widened and he leaned forward. "Nobody else was in the house, just like I said, but something threw a book at me."

"What book was it?" I whispered. I held tightly to the gris-gris and to the *Favorite Tales of Edgar Allan Poe*.

"I don't know," Jonathan said. "It doesn't matter, does it? What I'm saying is that something threw that book, and then all sorts of things started happening."

"I don't think—" Mom began.

"Tell them, Jonathan," Mrs. Lord said, looking even more pleased with herself.

"Okay. There was a kind of wind that blew through the room. I knew that there wasn't even a breeze that night, let alone something stronger. Then I heard whispering, like someone was saying a certain word over and over and over."

I gasped and managed to ask, "What word?"

"It doesn't matter," Mom said. "Let's drop this story right now."

But Jonathan acted as if he didn't hear Mom. He said to me, "I don't know what the word was. I probably could have figured it out if I'd listened carefully, but I didn't try because I made the mistake of shining the beam of my flashlight up to the ceiling. That's when I nearly dropped dead of fright, because there were all these horrible heads making faces at me—sticking out their tongues and whispering. I jumped up and ran back to the kitchen, and all the way I could feel something like fingers pulling at my face and hair."

Mom's nose and cheeks had turned pink, and her eyes sparked with anger. I knew she was having trouble keeping her feelings under control. She stepped up to face Jonathan, who gulped and stepped back. "Let me guess what comes next. You climbed out of the window and ran home."

Jonathan nodded. "That's about it."

"And told your story to your grandmother."

"And to my parents and my friends. I guess I told it to anyone who'd listen."

I suppose Mom could see that Jonathan had

thought we'd be an eager audience because he looked puzzled and hurt that she hadn't appreciated his story. She softened and even managed a smile. "Jonathan," she said. "You were ten years old at the time."

He sounded defensive. "Old enough to know and remember what I saw."

"Of course you were," Mom said. "But you had heard the stories about the house over and over before that night, hadn't you?"

"Yes."

"I think you said that your grandmother had told you what Charlotte had written in her diary."

"That's right. Are you trying to tell me I imagined everything I saw and heard?"

"You were swept into your experience through the power of suggestion. You were frightened. You were receptive. You saw and heard and felt exactly what had been described to you."

"It really happened," Jonathan insisted.

"You *think* it did," Mom said, firmly but gently.

Now it was Jonathan's turn to get exasperated. "What's the difference between *it happened* and thinking it happened?"

"One's based in reality. One isn't," Mom explained.

"I still don't—"

"Thinking it happened, when it didn't, affects only you," Mom said. "It means the experience won't be repeated by others."

"But there were others."

Mom's voice had a calm, patient tone. I hated it when she was deliberately calm and patient with me, and I knew Jonathan probably didn't like it either. "The bottom line, Jonathan, is that we don't believe in ghosts," Mom said.

She turned to Mrs. Lord, who had stopped looking smug, and told her, "We can't be frightened away from Graymoss. We have great plans for it. When the house has been modernized, with new paint and wallpaper, and we've moved in with our daughter and new family of adopted children, Derek and I hope that you'll come to visit."

Mrs. Lord's face twisted painfully. "This house could provide a treasure trove of history."

Mom smiled broadly. "This house will provide a home for our wonderful children."

*How about me?* I thought. *Why doesn't it matter what I think?*

Mrs. Lord hadn't given up. She got busy telling Mom something, so I nudged Jonathan and said in a low voice, "Would you please show me the window with the broken lock?"

We worked our way back to the kitchen, which was bright with noon sunlight. Every crack in the plastered walls and every smudge on the fireplace stood out in detail. The large room had cupboards on its outside wall, and three doors on the wall that faced it. "I wish there was food in this place," Jonathan said. "I'm hungry." He opened a door to a pantry lined with shelves, but the shelves were empty.

"I'm hungry, too," I answered.

The door to the butler's pantry stood open, but the third door was shut. I tried the handle, but it was locked.

Jonathan nodded toward the low hum of voices in the entry hall. "If they're going to be talking for a while, we could borrow Grandma's car and get something to eat. Would you like that?"

"I don't think my parents will let me. We were about to drive to Baton Rouge," I said.

The moment the words were out of my mouth I wanted to bang my head against the wall. What was the matter with me? Why couldn't I be cool and smiling and say, "Sure." *I don't think my parents will let me* . . . I sounded like I was five years old.

"Okay," Jonathan said as if he didn't care one way or another.

Maybe he thought *I* didn't care. I had to say something to make things right, so I gulped down the tightness in my throat and added, "Maybe next time . . . if you still want to."

"Sure, but I doubt there will be a next time. I mean, after your mother's in this house at night just once—"

"If I try hard enough, I think I can talk her into coming back tonight," I said.

He chuckled. "Tonight? Good for you. That's fast work."

I didn't know what Jonathan thought was so funny. I continued, "I almost forgot what we came for. Which window did you climb in?"

Jonathan walked to a low-set window next to the back door and examined the bottom sash. "It's right here," he said. "This one where the cord's frayed through. Nobody's ever fixed it. There's still a gap at the bottom." He raised the sash as high as it would go, and it held.

*The window's been broken for seven or eight years, and it hasn't been fixed?* The thought seemed

98

strange. "Did you close the window when you left?" I asked, suddenly very curious.

Jonathan scrunched up his forehead, thinking hard. I noticed that, even with a wrinkled forehead, Jonathan was really good-looking.

"I can't remember," he answered. "I was only ten years old. I was scared out of my mind. I was moving fast. But I knew I was doing something I shouldn't. Probably I stopped long enough to slam down the window 'cause I didn't want to get caught."

"Were your friends still waiting for you?" I asked.

Jonathan grinned. "No. They weren't going to stick around any longer than necessary. Besides, their parents would have come looking for them."

"I bet they gave you a bad time for not staying all night in the house."

"They tried, but it didn't last long because none of them were brave enough to do even as much as I'd done." Jonathan leaned against a stained wooden table and studied me. "I'm sorry the house is haunted. We'd go to the same high school and we could get to know each other."

I felt my face grow hot, I was so embarrassed. Girls in the books I read didn't have any trouble talking to guys. Why couldn't I? Finally I asked, "Do you live in Bogue City?" just to fill the silence.

"My dad's an attorney here, and my mom teaches first grade," Jonathan said.

"Does your grandmother live with you?"

He laughed. "Not on your life. Grandma's too used to running things the way she wants them.

99

She likes to get her own way. I'm betting that she wears down your parents and gets Graymoss for her historical society."

I spoke before I thought. "I wish she would."

Jonathan tilted his head and studied me. "Don't you like the idea of living here?"

I hedged. "I like Graymoss. I really do. But it's hard to imagine what it would be like if a dozen or more kids were also living here."

"You're an only child? So am I," Jonathan said. But he smiled and added, "Sometimes I used to wish I had a couple of brothers. Maybe having other kids in the family wouldn't be so bad."

"Maybe it would."

Jonathan shrugged. "Like I told you, when the awful things happen in this house at night, your parents are bound to change their minds."

"They wouldn't believe me when I told them what happened in Placide Blevins's bedroom. Mom thinks I've been influenced by Charlotte's diary and things I've read about ghosts and that's why I saw . . ." I stopped, but Jonathan prodded.

"Saw what? You can tell me."

Jonathan's nice eyes were deep and warm. I decided to trust him. "When we were in Placide Blevins's bedroom there was a depression, like the body of a man, right in the middle of the bed. I saw it."

"You're telling me you really saw a ghost?" Jonathan's eyes widened in amazement.

"What are you so surprised about?" I asked him. "You told us about the ghostly things that happened to you."

For just a moment Jonathan looked flustered,

but he pulled himself together. "You're right. I just didn't think that you . . . Go on. Did anything else happen?"

"A book fell out of the bookcase onto my shoulder." I held out *Favorite Tales of Edgar Allan Poe*.

Jonathan's look of amazement quickly turned into a cynical smile. "What kind of game are you playing, Lia?"

I stared at him in surprise. "Game? What are you talking about? You asked me to tell you what had happened to me, and I trusted you and told you."

Jonathan walked to one end of the kitchen and back again. He stopped and put his hands on my shoulders. "Okay, Lia," he said. "I didn't figure you out right. What you just told me about the book was so much like what had happened to me it kind of took me by surprise, that's all. Come on. Let's go out on the veranda. I'd like to get out of here."

As he took my left hand and began to lead me toward the back door, the bag of gris-gris swung freely under my shirt.

"Jonathan," I began, but whatever else I'd planned to say flew out of my mind. I yelped as the window slammed down with a bang.

101

# CHAPTER TEN

Jonathan grinned down at me, and I realized I had wrapped my arms around him in a stranglehold. "I'm sorry," I said, and backed away as quickly as I could.

"I'm not," Jonathan answered, and his eyes twinkled. "Any time you get scared and want to do that again, I'm available."

"I guess all our talk about ghosts and evil things made me jumpy. I shouldn't have been spooked by a broken window sash."

"I meant what I said," he told me. He pulled a card out of his pocket and handed it to me. "This is my dad's business card, but it's got our home phone number on it, too. Call me if you need me." He smiled warmly. "Call me anyway. Let me know when you're coming back. Okay?"

I smiled in return and dropped the card into the

pocket of my shirt. "Okay," I said. I hoped Jonathan couldn't read my mind to know I thought it was more than okay. It was great, terrific, tremendous, fantastic.

Mrs. Lord's voice warbled, "Jonathan? Where are you?"

"Gotta go, Lia," Jonathan said. He strode ahead through the dining room and into the entry hall. I followed happily. Broad shoulders and long legs . . . Jonathan looked great coming or going.

Mrs. Lord was pleasant as she said goodbye, and Mom seemed calm, so I guessed neither of them had become too upset about the other's plans for Graymoss.

We watched the Lords drive away; then Dad looked at his watch. "Let's take a quick look at the outbuildings before we head back to Baton Rouge."

"Wait a minute," Mom said. She dug through her purse, then handed it to me to hold. "My tape measure—I just remembered that I left it upstairs."

"I'll get it," Dad said, but Mom shook her head.

"I know right where it is. I'll only be a second."

As soon as Mom went back into the house, Dad looked at his watch. "It's going to be a long second," he said, and chuckled. "She'll take another look at the bedrooms and count how many bunk beds will fit, and think about wallpaper. We might as well make ourselves comfortable."

But, as we settled down on the top step, Mom ran through the open front door. She leaned against the side of the house, breathing rapidly.

Dad got up and smiled at her. "We didn't expect you to set a speed record."

I saw something in Mom's face that Dad hadn't noticed. "What scared you?" I asked her.

As Mom looked at me the fear in her eyes changed to a kind of tenderness. "The same thing that frightened you, honey," she said. "The diary, the stories, the rumors . . . the power of suggestion. That's all it was."

"But, Mom—"

"Lia," she said, "I understand *why* you were frightened. I—I gave in to the feelings myself."

"You didn't say what you saw, or what you heard, or—"

"And I'm not going to. Subject closed." Mom walked ahead of us down the front steps and handed the house keys to Mr. Boudreau, who was waiting for us on the drive. "I'd like to get duplicates of those keys," she said.

Mr. Boudreau nodded. "Wait a little while afore you go to the expense," he said in a doomsday voice. "You might not be needin' 'em."

Mom just shook her head and didn't say anything. I guess she felt she had argued enough.

We toured the vegetable garden, which brightened Mom's spirits so much that she again began to make plans for an even larger garden. I remembered the year she grew zucchini. The vines produced so many we had zucchini in everything, including bread and cake. Ever since then, I've cringed when I've seen a zucchini. I hoped zucchini wasn't on her list.

Next we looked over what remained of the summer kitchen—a kind of shed with open walls, set on a cement slab, with some of the supports and most of the roof missing.

"Stay away from it, Lia," Dad said, as if I'd had any intention of ever going inside it. "That place is an accident waiting to happen."

The privy was a hopeless mess of fallen walls and collapsed roof. I didn't want to look at it.

The barn was okay, I guess. At least, it wasn't as beat up as the other outbuildings, and there weren't more than a few gaps in the walls. But Dad said, "We don't need a barn or stables. I suggest that we have the whole thing torn down and erect a good-sized toolshed and workshop in its place."

Mom nodded. "Keeping horses would be fun for the kids, but it's way out of our price range."

*So are all those kids,* I wanted to tell her, but I kept my mouth shut.

Mr. Boudreau shoved his hands into his pockets and leaned against what remained of a dead oak, its top branches gone and its trunk nothing but splinters of wood pointing up to the sky. "Couple of these old trees could come out, while you're at it, *if* you're at it," he said.

"No 'if's,' " Mom told him. "We'll talk to the structural engineers who are going to examine the house. As soon as we get their evaluation, we'll begin work on modernizing the kitchen and adding bathrooms. Then you and I will have a long talk about expanding the vegetable garden and putting playground equipment in this open field ahead of us." She turned to Dad and smiled. "Do you think we could fit a baseball diamond in that far corner?"

Before Dad could answer, Mr. Boudreau shook his head and said, "I wouldn't, if I was you. Kids

105

playin' and yellin' back there might be a bother to your renter."

We all looked at him with surprise. "What renter?" Mom asked.

"There's an old cabin on y'all's property, back in the trees. You can't see it good from here, but it's there. Where the overseers once lived, I'm guessin'. The old wooden slave quarters fell apart years ago, but that cabin was built a whole lot better, and Ava Phipps has been livin' there for a good long while."

A tingle ran up my backbone when Mr. Boudreau mentioned the overseers. The last overseer had been Morgan Slade. That was where he had lived. The story in Charlotte's diary was beginning to come more and more alive to me.

"Does anyone else know about this Ava Phipps living on the property?" Mom asked.

"You mean, like is Miz Phipps a squatter or is she livin' there legal?" Mr. Boudreau asked.

"Yes. That's what I mean," Mom said.

"Your grandmother knew," Mr. Boudreau said. "I guess you could say that at first Miz Phipps was a squatter. I mean, she come across this empty cabin, and she moved right in and stayed. I knew about it, but I wasn't about to chase her off, considering her circumstances.

"I told Mrs. Langley when she came here to check on how things were going, and she and Miz Phipps sat down and had them a long talk. They was both a lot younger then, but Miz Phipps . . . well, she never was quite right in the head. Mrs. Langley was a kind woman. She didn't turn Miz Phipps out, 'cause where would the poor woman go? Mrs. Langley told Miz Phipps she could go on livin' in that cabin and nobody would bother her."

He looked at Mom questioningly, and she came through. I knew she would.

"Grandma was like that," Mom said. "And I'll be glad to carry out her wishes. Mrs. Phipps can live in the cabin, but I do want to talk to her. She needs to know what our plans are for the house."

Mr. Boudreau just shrugged, as if he were positive those plans would never take shape. "Y'all got on the right kind of shoes for walkin' in the field," he said. "When you get into the field, you'll see a kind of path that runs along the edge of the woods under the trees. Take it and it'll lead you right to the cabin."

We followed his directions to a narrow beaten path, and somehow I found myself leading a single file, with Mom behind me and Dad behind her. The path skirted the field and was shaded by the tall pines and thick vines and underbrush that were tangled together to create a wall of woods.

As we walked more deeply into shadow a pair of gleaming eyes just over my head startled me. I stopped short, and Mom bumped into me. As we caught our balance a large, black, furry animal on an overhead branch hissed and spit, then leaped from the branch into the underbrush.

"What in the world was that?" Mom asked.

"Just a cat," I said. "But it didn't act like a cat. Maybe it was frightened. I don't know if we scared it as much as it scared me."

"Some people dump kittens in lonely places, instead of taking them to animal shelters that will find them homes," Dad said. "That cat may have learned to fend for itself when it was still a kitten so it has grown up wild."

"Poor thing," I said. "Maybe we could bring food for it."

Even though I realized there'd be nothing for a cat to eat at the house, I automatically glanced back. There was no sign of the house. The woods had curved inward, shutting out the rest of the world. We were in a deep green silence, without even the caw of a grackle or the scold of a mockingbird. I was used to city sounds, so I felt as if we had landed in an alien country.

I guess Mom and Dad felt the same because we walked on in silence, the beaten grass muffling the sound of our footsteps. I kept searching the depths of the underbrush, though, wary of once again coming across that unfriendly cat.

Suddenly a large gray-striped cat shot across my path, racing from a clump of high grass, where it had been hidden, into a break in the bushes. I looked to see where it had disappeared and discovered a small clearing just the other side of the break. Within the clearing stood a cabin made of bricks.

The cabin was square, with a chimney rising at each end. A wooden porch, which stretched the length of the cabin, was supported by five short piles of mortared bricks. Two posts, which were anchored on the porch, held up a steeply slanting, badly patched roof. There should have been three posts, but one at the far end was missing, and there the roof dipped and sagged. One door and one window opened onto the porch, and a rectangular window, covered by a sheet of plastic, filled the space at the side of the fireplace. Two cats rested on the porch, one sat in the window, and the gray-striped cat perched on the roof.

"There it is," I said. I forced my way through the low shrubbery, bending to push away branches, and stepped into the clearing. "There's Morgan Slade's house."

"Whose?" Dad asked as he came up behind me.

"Morgan Slade is someone out of the past. The woman who lives here is Ava Phipps," Mom said.

The door creaked open, and a tiny woman peered out, as if she'd heard her name. She squinted, holding her head up as if it were hard for her to see, and called in a squeaky voice, "Who are you?"

"I'm Anne Starling," Mom said, "the new owner of Graymoss, and this is my husband, Derek, and my daughter, Lia. We came to meet you."

"New owner?" Mrs. Phipps looked a little frightened. "Better come on inside," she said.

Up close she was even smaller. She reminded me of a sparrow, with her little round head and tiny bones. She waved us to a lumpy, dark sofa with some of its springs and upholstery missing, and she perched on a ladder-back chair, her legs dangling. The black cat we'd seen earlier leaped onto her lap and lay there, watching us. He kept his nonblinking, gleaming eyes on us—a silent watchcat. The gray-striped cat climbed through an open window and settled on top of a cupboard.

Mom told Mrs. Phipps about Sarah's death.

Then, for a while, the two of them talked about the good weather and Mrs. Phipps's six cats. I looked around the room, wondering if it still contained traces of the horrible Morgan Slade, who had run off with the Blevinses' valuables and threatened to run off with Charlotte, too. But the unpainted walls were bare, and the unsanded board shelves by the fireplace were piled with old cooking utensils, three dented metal teakettles, and a hodgepodge of odds and ends. *Things that belong in a dump,* I thought, until with a wave of guilt I realized that was probably where they had come from. The room had a damp, musty smell that mingled with the scents of strong coffee and stale grease. In spite of the uncurtained windows, it was a dark, gloomy box, cut off from the sun.

Mom began telling Mrs. Phipps about the plans she and Dad had for making a home. Mrs. Phipps listened, her head tilted the way sparrows tilt their heads, until Mom paused. Then Mrs. Phipps said, "Too much noise. Workers, children. I don't like it."

"You won't hear the sounds of construction. The house is far enough away, and the woods will cut off any noise. As far as the children are concerned, we'll teach them to respect your territory."

"Won't do no good," Mrs. Phipps said.

Looking surprised, Mom answered, "Yes, it will. If we give the children love and security and a happy home—"

Mrs. Phipps interrupted. "That's not what I'm talking about. I mean you can't live in that house, not with the evil in it."

Mom gave a discouraged sigh, but I leaned forward eagerly.

"Tell us about the evil," I said. "Have you seen it?"

"What's to tell?" Mrs. Phipps asked. "It's there. Everybody around here knows so."

"It seems that everyone around here has been filled with the same wild stories," Mom said. "But they don't affect us. We don't believe in ghosts, Mrs. Phipps."

"Don't matter if you believe in them or not. If they're there, they're there," Mrs. Phipps said.

Dad chuckled. "Good point," he said. "We just won't let them bother us. Okay?"

Mrs. Phipps leaned forward, clutching the sides of her chair for balance. "They'll bother you whether you like it or not," she said. "And they'll keep on bothering you until they feel free to leave."

"They're free to leave anytime they want," Dad said.

"It's not that easy," Mrs. Phipps said. She was leaning forward so far I was afraid she'd fall out of her chair. This time she twisted slightly to stare at me with her tiny bird eyes. "There's only one way to set a ghost free, and that's find out what's making it hang around. Ghosts haunt a place because they've got a reason. When you find the reason, then you can set about putting the ghost's mind at ease so it can leave."

The woman in the voodoo shop in New Orleans had said almost the same thing. "Mrs. Phipps," I said, "Placide Blevins was shot before he could tell Charlotte what he had on his mind. Is that what you mean? That he still has something he needs to tell?"

"Placide wasn't evil. He isn't the horror that lives in the house," Mrs. Phipps answered. "Placide may have unfinished business, but he would never have frightened his loving granddaughter like that. And he wouldn't have scared other people to death."

Mom got a determined gleam in her eye. "No one has been able to tell us the identities of the people who were supposedly frightened to death or the circumstances surrounding their deaths. Do you know the facts?"

Mrs. Phipps nodded. "Just that it happened. That's enough facts to suit me." She glanced at the book in my hand. "I see Placide Blevins gave you that book."

I jumped with surprise and hoped Mom and Dad wouldn't start asking questions. "Why did you say that?" I asked her.

"Because once his spirit tried to give it to me," she said. "It didn't do no good because my eyes are too old and tired for reading now, so I give it back."

I had a dozen questions. "You've been in the house then? In the daytime? Or at night?"

"Both," Mrs. Phipps said. "In the daytime it's mostly peaceful, but after dark things turn ugly. There's scary faces and whispers and fingers that pull at you and—"

Mom broke in. "Mrs. Phipps," she said, "Mrs. Lord told me that she read Charlotte's diary. You seem to be familiar with the contents, too. Did

112

Mrs. Lord by any chance make a copy of the diary?"

"She typed it word for word," Mrs. Phipps said, "and it wasn't by chance. It was on purpose. She's got it up on display in that little historical museum in Bogue City."

"Have you read it?"

"Oh, yes," Mrs. Phipps said. "That's what give me the idea to come here. I knew nobody was likely to want to live in the house. I looked around the property, and sure enough, here sat an empty cabin, ready for the moving in."

Mom wouldn't give up. "The events you described in the house are the same as the events Charlotte described in her diary," she said.

Mrs. Phipps's head bobbed in agreement. "The very same."

Mom looked flustered and shifted uncomfortably on the sofa. "What I'm trying to say is that the diary influenced you."

"Probably did," Mrs. Phipps said.

Mom relaxed and smiled. "There. You see. The power of suggestion," she said.

"No, the power in that house wasn't suggesting anything," Mrs. Phipps answered. "With all those goings-on, it was saying flat out, 'Get out of here, if you know what's good for you.' It influenced me right out of that house."

Mrs. Phipps pointed at a large oil lamp with tiny roses painted on the globe. "I'll come straight out with it," she said. "I went to the house just to look around 'cause I was curious. I found a broken window sash, so I decided to climb inside and see if there was anything I might use. I found that lamp and liked it. Nobody else was using it, so I didn't think anybody would care if I borrowed it. I always meant to write to that nice Mrs. Langley and tell her I'd take good care of her lamp and give it back if she wanted it, but I'm not much of a one for writing letters. Anyway, I never got around to buying a stamp."

"It's all right, Mrs. Phipps," Mom said. "You can have the lamp."

Mrs. Phipps hunched her shoulders and narrowed her eyes. "I borrowed two pans and a kettle, too."

"You may keep them."

Mrs. Phipps smiled a broad, gap-toothed smile. "You're a nice lady," she said. "Nice as your grandmother. I'm sorry you won't be around long."

"But I will be around," Mom said. "Remember? I told you our plans for the house."

"I heard what *you* said," Mrs. Phipps answered. "But maybe you didn't hear what *I* said. I pointed out that there'd be no living in that house until you put the evil to rest."

I could see that Mom was having trouble keeping her cool. "Mrs. Phipps, I'm not about to—"

Mrs. Phipps interrupted. "I never figured you would, Miz Starling. I can tell you right now that closing your mind off the way you do, you'd never be able to do it." She turned her gaze on me. "But you can do it, girl. I can see that. You're the one. Find the reason the evil is there, and maybe then you can send it away."

"Why me?" I asked. I held my breath, frightened of this strange woman, as I waited for her answer.

114

Mom lost it. "I can't imagine why we're having this conversation!" she snapped. "As I told you, Mrs. Phipps, we don't believe in ghosts."

"Your girl does," Mrs. Phipps said.

"No, Lia doesn't," Mom insisted.

Mrs. Phipps glanced at the neckline of my shirt, then back into my eyes. "I think you do believe," she said to me. "Else why are you protecting yourself with gris-gris?"

# CHAPTER ELEVEN

I quickly glanced down and saw that the bag on the string around my neck had shifted and had fallen outside the neckline of my shirt. It had probably happened while I was bending over, trying to get into the clearing. I was glad Mrs. Phipps was the only one who had looked at me. I dropped the little bag of gris-gris down inside my shirt again, thankful that my parents were still intent on Mrs. Phipps and not on me. I couldn't think of an answer.

It didn't matter, because Mom stood up. "Mrs. Phipps, we've been hearing a great many silly ghost stories about Graymoss from everyone we've met here," she said. Her voice was controlled because she was trying to be polite, but I could tell she was steaming. "I don't want Lia to be drawn into believing there is some kind of evil in the house. This business of protecting herself from ghosts with—well, whatever it was you were talking about . . ."

I smothered a sigh of relief. Apparently Mom didn't know about voodoo charms, and I supposed Dad didn't, either, because he hadn't reacted to the mention of gris-gris. He put an arm around Mom's shoulders and nudged her toward the door.

"We enjoyed meeting you, Mrs. Phipps," he said.

In the open doorway Mom collected herself enough to say, "As I promised, no one will disturb you, Mrs. Phipps. And if you need anything, please don't hesitate to ask."

The gray-striped cat leaped to the arm of the sofa and peered into my face as though asking why I was still sitting there like an open-mouthed statue. I jumped up and made a dash after my parents, who by this time had crossed the porch. "Goodbye, Mrs. Phipps," I said.

In spite of her small size she was as fast as I was. Suddenly she was at my side, clutching my arm with her little bird-bone fingers. "I don't know how good that gris-gris you've got is gonna work or how long its power will last," she said in a low voice. "Find the reason the evil is in that house. That's the only way you're ever going to get rid of it."

What made her think I wanted to get rid of it? Getting rid of the evil did *not* fit into my plans. I pulled away from Mrs. Phipps's grip and caught up with my parents. I was careful this time to keep the gris-gris hidden.

Mom strode back to our car double time. Dad and I could hardly keep up with her.

"We all need something to eat," Dad said. "Should we try that cafe we passed in Bogue City?"

"No!" Mom boomed as she slid into the front passenger seat and slammed the car door. "I don't want to talk to one more person around here. They're all trying to get us to go away." I heard her snuffle, and she rubbed hard at her nose. "We *won't* go away! We're going to make a home here."

Dad turned on the ignition, and I settled back for the ride into Baton Rouge, tucking my book into a pocket on the back of the front seat. But we all jumped as someone tapped at Mom's window and a craggy face with a lopsided smile appeared.

Mom quickly rolled down the window, and the man leaned in. "Not leaving, are you?" he asked.

"Yes, we are," Mom said.

"But you can't . . . at least not until we've come to some kind of an understanding," the man said.

"Who are you?" Mom asked, spacing the words slowly as though she were trying extra hard to be patient. "And what kind of understanding are you talking about?"

The man grinned and pulled off the sweat-stained Panama hat he was wearing. "Sorry about that. I should have introduced myself right off. I'm Homer Tavey."

Dad remembered the name. "The antiques dealer," he said.

"You heard of me?" Mr. Tavey beamed.

"Yes. From Mrs. Lord."

Mr. Tavey's happy expression quickly disappeared. "Don't pay any mind to anything Hannah told you. She's scared you're gonna sell some of your furnishings to me, and she wants to get her hands on them for that little historical society of hers."

"We're not selling anything, Mr. Tavey," Mom said.

He looked surprised. "You can get a nice price for the house and property from Ray Merle, and I'll give you the best offer you can get for the furnishings. I know a lady upriver who's been dying to get her hands on a genuine antique tester bed. She'd probably go for a highboy, too."

"I'm sorry to spoil your hopes, Mr. Tavey," Mom said, "but I repeat, nothing in this house is for sale. My husband and daughter and I are going to live in Graymoss."

Mr. Tavey looked shocked. "I seriously doubt that," he said.

Mom spoke through clenched teeth. "I don't want to hear one more story about evil things in the house or ghosts haunting the place."

"You haven't been here at night—" Mr. Tavey began, but Mom cut him off.

"Have you?"

"No, but everybody knows that—"

"Goodbye, Mr. Tavey," Mom said, and jabbed at the button that rolled up the window. "Let's go," she said to Dad. "Right this minute. If one more neighbor shows up I'm going to scream!"

We took off and drove through Bogue City

without stopping. When we reached the highway, Mom finally began to relax.

"Do you realize," she asked, "that everyone who has told us about ghosts has an ulterior motive for wanting us to leave? Mrs. Lord wants us to donate the house to her historical society. Mr. Merle wants the property for a housing development. Mrs. Phipps wants to be left in peace. And Mr. Tavey wants our antiques."

"What about Mr. Boudreau?" I asked. "He talked about the hauntings, too."

"If we moved in, Mr. Boudreau would have a great deal more work to do. Plus the fact that he and his wife would lose their vegetable garden. I'm sure he'd be glad to keep the status quo."

It was now or never. I was ready with my zinger. "You know what you have to do, Mom," I said. "You have to prove to all of them that you're right and they're wrong. We have to go back to Graymoss tonight."

For a while Mom didn't answer. Then she said, "Maybe you're right, Lia. Maybe I do. I'll give it some thought."

I hugged my arms and tried to keep from grinning, just in case Dad glanced in the rearview mirror and saw me. At that moment I knew how Mom felt when she clapped her hands in excitement and happiness, because—dorky or not—I would have liked to do the same thing.

I was sure that if Mom spent the night at Graymoss, it would be the last time she'd want to set foot in the house. She'd been scared once, but talked herself out of it. She wouldn't be able to do that if the ghost let go and gave her a night filled with horror. We wouldn't move, I'd still see Jolie every day, and I could read in my room in peace without a dozen noisy kids driving me crazy. Thanks to the haunts who frightened everyone away from Graymoss, *I* was going to win—not Mom!

By the time we slipped into a booth in a fast-food restaurant in Baton Rouge, Mom was cranky, Dad's sense of humor had vanished, and I was starving. But it's amazing the magic that hamburgers and Cokes can do.

Dad leaned back, sipping his Coke, and began making up silly For Sale signs for Graymoss. " 'Three floors of loveliness. Creeps in the cellar, ghosts in the garage—' "

"There isn't a garage," Mom said, and giggled.

"Don't spoil my ad," Dad said. " 'Haunts in the hallways, bats in the bedroom—' "

"And no bats," Mom interrupted. "You can be prosecuted for fraudulent advertising."

They both laughed. Dad took Mom's hand and said, "Then we'd better not try to sell the house. We'll just have to live in it."

The joy in Mom's face made me feel terrible. I looked away. I hated to spoil her dream, but there *were* ghosts no one could live with, and the sooner she found out about it the better.

"What are we going to do now?" I asked. "Go home and come back to Graymoss this evening?"

Mom and Dad gave each other one of those

secret looks that kids aren't supposed to see. It meant that they had something in mind for me. Probably something I wouldn't like.

Mom smiled at me and said, "We'll drive home in a little while, but we have a stop to make first."

I had a look of my own. I rolled my eyes skyward, sighed, and said, "Am I supposed to guess where?"

"Lighten up," Dad said good-naturedly. "Give your mother a chance to tell you."

"Through my job I've often been in contact with the director of the Adelaide Barker Home for Children in Baton Rouge," Mom said. Eagerly she leaned across the table toward me. "I've visited the children, and the director knows about our dream. Lia, honey, you've made it clear that you have reservations about what your father and I want to do. We think if you meet the children you'll become as enthusiastic as we are about moving into Graymoss with a large family—children no one has wanted to adopt. Do you want me to tell you how the adoptions work?"

I hedged. "Right now?"

"Now's as good a time as any," Mom said. "This is the situation. We'll visit the home a number of times. We'll get to know the children, and they'll get to know us. We'll begin to figure out which children will join us—"

"They have more than a dozen? How many kids live there?"

"Usually around sixty to seventy-five. The home has a very low rate of adoption—something like only twenty-seven percent—because most people want babies. They don't want older children, or an entire family of brothers and sisters who hope to stay together, or children with physical or mental handicaps."

"I know. You already told me all that," I said. I slumped against the back of the booth. Mom was making me feel worse.

"All right. Next step," she said. "We'll sign up and begin the paperwork that will result in a license to be adoptive parents. We'll have to take parenting classes—"

"But you *are* parents. You have *me!*"

"Of course we do, honey, but the rules and regulations don't take that into consideration."

"That's all I am? Just something that doesn't count under a rule and regulation?"

Dad took one of my hands. "Not to us," he said. "You're the most important part of our lives, Lia."

*Then think about what you're doing to me,* I thought, but I didn't say anything.

Mom waited a moment, then went on explaining. "We'll go through a police check and a visit from one or more social workers. They'll all prepare reports on us. The reports will be given to the children's caseworkers. If all goes well, by the time the workers have finished putting in electricity, and digging a new water well, and adding a modern kitchen and bathrooms to Graymoss, our new family will be ready to be adopted."

"That could take months and months." I tried to keep from sounding hopeful.

Dad sighed and said, "There are so many kids who badly need homes, but unfortunately, there's a lot of time-consuming red tape and paperwork to get through."

123

Both Mom and Dad looked at me expectantly. I knew they were still waiting for me to say something cheerful and encouraging. But that wasn't the way I felt, and I couldn't fake it. "Why do you want to go there and get the kids' hopes up until you're positive that . . . that . . ."

Mom sat up straight. "Don't start with that evil-in-the-house business. I don't want to hear another word about ghosts. Your father and I will go to Graymoss tonight and prove to everyone that we're not going to be intimidated by a lot of stupid stories, and that will be the end of that."

I grabbed at the first thought that came into my mind. Trying to look indignant, I said, "I was going to point out that the structural engineers haven't even been to the house yet. You don't know that Graymoss can be lived in."

Dad smiled. "Don't let it worry you. I did some checking on my own while we were there. The house was built to last. I'm sure the engineers will agree."

"Were you down in the basement?" I asked. "I know there's a basement, because I could see the little windows at ground level." I eagerly slid upright. "You know, sometimes a basement can develop rot and mildew."

Dad laughed so loudly that the people in the next booth turned around to see what was so funny. "Give it up, Lia," he said. "The door to the basement was locked, so I didn't go down to examine it, but I'm not worried. I've been in enough of these old plantation homes to know how solid their basements and foundations are—"

It suddenly dawned on me what Mom had said.

"Wait a minute," I interrupted. "Mom, you just told me that you and Dad were going to Graymoss tonight. What about me? I want to go, too."

Dad shook his head. "I think it will be much better if you and your vivid imagination stay home. Talk on the phone to Jolie. Watch a good movie. We won't be long."

"But I *have* to be there with you," I insisted.

"After the way you frightened yourself today in broad daylight? What would your imagination do to you in the dark? We're not going to find out," Mom said.

"I'm not a child," I argued. They couldn't go without me! I *had* to be there to see what the evil would do in its full fury. "Look, I'm fifteen," I said. "I'm not going to be afraid."

"It's been decided," Dad told me.

Mom picked up her purse and slid out of the booth. "Let's go visit the Barker Home," she said. "I can't wait to begin finding our kids."

# CHAPTER TWELVE

The Adelaide Barker Home for Children didn't look like a home. It was a large redbrick building on a busy street. The front door opened into a large, bright room that looked like the lobby of a business office, with vinyl-covered sofas and chairs and fake plants. But no public lobby would have eight kids draped all over two big sofas or lying on their stomachs in front of the TV, watching noisy cartoons.

At one side of the room was a glassed-in office. A tall, gray-haired woman popped out of the door that was labeled OFFICE OF THE DIRECTOR and strode toward Mom with outstretched arms. "I'm so glad to see you, Anne," she said, raising her voice over the sound from the television. She briefly hugged Mom and shook hands with Dad.

"Barbara, this is our daughter, Lia," Mom said. "Lia, this is Mrs. Lane."

A couple of the kids had twisted around to stare at us, and I felt awkward and uncomfortable as I shook Mrs. Lane's hand.

"What an exciting venture this must be for you, Lia!" she said with a smile.

All I could do was nod at her and wish Mom and Dad and the kids who were staring would get interested in something besides me. I could feel myself blushing, and I hated it.

Without pausing for breath, Mrs. Lane called out, "Dillon, turn down the volume, please. Anne, Derek, why don't you come into my office where we can talk?" and "Lia, you'll probably want to meet some of the other children. Just feel free to look around."

*Other children? Oh, sure.* As Mom and Dad followed Mrs. Lane into her office, I angrily clamped my teeth together and sat down on an empty chair away from the others and close to the front door.

A little girl, who didn't look any older than seven, detached herself from the group that had turned back to watching the cartoons. She walked directly to me and leaned closer to study my face with huge black eyes. "How do you do that?" she asked.

"Do what?" I mumbled.

"Make your face get all red, like it was a minute ago." She shook her head, the ends of her braids bouncing. "Do it again," she said.

"I can't," I told her, trying to keep a straight face. "It happens when I get embarrassed."

Her nose wrinkled. "Like when you get called on in school and you lose your place? Or when you wait too long to run for the bathroom and you don't make it?"

I laughed. I couldn't help it. But she didn't seem to mind. "My name's Lia. What's yours?" I asked her.

"Demetria," she said. "I'm nine years old, and I'm here with my brother and sister. How come you're here? Did you get kicked out of your foster home?"

I shook my head, and Demetria said, "We did. But it wasn't my fault. It was Robbie's fault. He couldn't take our foster mother yellin' at Delia anymore, so he threw her best china platter on the floor and it broke. Our foster mother yelled some more and said that was the last straw and she didn't want such bad kids in her house one more day. So Mrs. Lane came and got us and brought us here." Demetria shook her head sadly. "We aren't really bad kids," she said. "Robbie just didn't like all that yellin'. And Delia makes lots of mistakes, but not on purpose."

"How old is Robbie?" I asked.

Demetria brightened. "He's seven," she said, "and Delia is four. Mrs. Lane said she was gonna try to keep us together. Do you have any brothers or sisters to keep together with?"

"No," I said, "but I have a mother and father."

For just an instant I could see a terrible longing in Demetria's eyes. But she gave a shake of her head and stood up as tall as she could. "We had a mother and father once," she said. "That counts for somethin'."

"That counts for a lot," I answered.

"Do you want to just sit here doin' nothin'?" Demetria asked. "Or do you want to come and see my house?"

"What house?"

"C'mon. I'll show you."

Demetria held out a hand, so I got up and walked with her down a hallway to what looked like a kindergarten room. "This is where I built my playhouse," she said, and she led me to one corner of the room behind an upright piano where some blocks were piled to make a low wall.

A small girl sat inside the enclosure, sucking her thumb. Her dress was stained and smelled of urine.

Demetria sighed and shook her head. "Delia, how come you didn't go to the bathroom?" she asked.

Delia tugged her thumb out of her mouth with a pop. "Don't know where it is," she said, then thrust her thumb back like a cork in a bottle.

"You gotta show Delia things over and over again," Demetria said in a low voice, as if she were one adult talking to another. "Our foster mother before last said Delia drove her right up the wall."

Holding out her hands to Delia, Demetria said, "C'mon, Delia. I'll take you to get cleaned up."

As Demetria gathered her sister into her arms she gave me a desperate look. "Don't you go away, Lia," she said. "I haven't showed you around yet."

I found a roll of paper towels on a nearby cupboard and wiped up the puddle Delia had left. Then I went in search of the bathroom Delia couldn't find, so that I could wash my hands.

129

Farther down the hallway was a door with a cow painted on it. I pushed it open, and a boy about ten years old called out, "Hey!" He limped out of the bathroom and stopped to face me.

"Whatcha doin' in the boys' bathroom?" he demanded.

"I didn't know it was the boys' bathroom," I said. "I thought it was for girls. It has a cow on it."

He snickered. "The cow's on that door across the hall," he said. This one's a bull. You sure are dumb."

I blushed again. "I wasn't paying attention. It looked like a cow to me."

I stepped back into the hallway so he could get past me. He seemed to be having a lot of trouble when he walked.

"Are you gonna work here?" he asked.

"No," I said. "I just came to visit."

His eyes lit up. "You gonna take a kid to adopt? Maybe you want me. I'm smart. I get good grades in school, and I know a lot of jokes."

"I'm too young to adopt a child," I told him. "I'm only fifteen."

"Uh-oh," he said. "They can't keep you in a foster home either, huh? What did you do to get in trouble?"

This kid had a big mouth and he was a little bit of a smart aleck, but I couldn't help liking him. "What's your name?" I asked.

"Jimmy," he said. "What's yours?"

"Lia. And I didn't get in trouble. I'm here with my parents on a visit."

"You got parents?" he asked, and there was such

longing on his face that I wanted to hug him. "I never had any—just an aunt and her boyfriend. After he kicked me down the stairs and the police took me to a hospital, I got sent to foster homes."

"Why couldn't you stay in the foster homes?" I asked.

"Sometimes I have bad nightmares, and I cry out, and it wakes people up so they don't get their good night's sleep." He looked down at the tips of his shoes. "And in the daytime I need more help than other kids do."

Then he looked up at me with a lopsided grin. "I forgot. You need help, too. You need help findin' the right bathroom." He pointed at the other door, the one with the cow painted on it. "There it is."

He turned and limped down the hallway. It hurt to watch the terrible effort he was making. Tears blurred my eyes, so I shoved my way through the door and scrubbed my hands as hard as I could in the low washbasin.

The door opened, and Mom came in. "We were looking for you," she said. She saw the tears on my cheeks and asked, "What's wrong, honey?"

I grabbed a fistful of paper towels, trying to dry my face and hands at the same time. "Kids shouldn't be hurt or have to live the way Jimmy lived, or Demetria, or Delia."

I threw myself into a storm of words and tears about adults who kicked children down the stairs or yelled at little ones who made mistakes.

Mom waited until I had finished. Then she put her arms around me, smoothing back my hair and murmuring soft, loving Mom things the way she did when I was younger. It felt good, and I thought for a minute that while I was growing older maybe she would have done more of this . . . if I'd let her.

Finally I stepped away. "I'm okay now. Thanks, Mom," I said, and splashed cold water on my face.

She held out a hand. "Let's find your father and Barbara. They were wondering where you'd disappeared to."

As we walked out into the hall I asked, "Mom, doesn't it hurt you to see kids like these?"

"It hurts more," Mom said, "to walk away and leave them."

I stopped and faced her. "You'd want to take somebody like the boy I met named Jimmy? He told me he has terrible nightmares and cries out at night."

"I know Jimmy. He needs a series of operations on his right leg." Mom nodded. "With someone to reassure him that he's loved, Jimmy might stop having nightmares."

"What about Delia? She doesn't seem very smart and isn't housebroken."

"Potty trained," Mom corrected, and smiled. "Delia really needs someone to care for her, doesn't she?"

Arguments zipped and zinged around in my mind like stray arrows. "If you adopt a houseful of kids, it's going to mean an awful lot of hard work," I said.

"That's right," Mom said. "For all of us."

Surprised, I countered, "And you'll lose sleep."

"We expect to."

"And there'll be a lot of noise and probably some arguments—even fistfights."

"Of course."

"Mom," I complained, "you aren't making this easy."

"Nothing about our plan is going to be easy," she said. "But the results are going to be worthwhile, and that's what counts."

I still didn't like Mom and Dad's idea about filling Graymoss with kids no one else would adopt. At the same time I didn't like *not* liking it, or leaving Jimmy and Demetria and Delia without parents to take care of them. But I wanted my parents to myself and my quiet life to stay the same . . . didn't I? "I think . . . ," I began, then groaned. "I don't know what I think."

Mom put an arm around my shoulders. "It takes time to sort things out," she said. "Let's say good-bye to some of the children and to Barbara."

But before we left I had a question for Mrs. Lane. "What will happen to Delia and Robbie and Demetria? Will they be sent to another foster home?"

"There are none available at the moment, and because of Delia's extra needs, there aren't many foster parents who'd take her."

"Then do they just keep living here?"

"We might try another foster home, but when children are rejected—well, it's awfully hard on them. They'll probably keep living here, or in other institutions, until they're eighteen."

*Institutions?* I shuddered.

Demetria appeared, leading Delia by the hand. Delia was wearing clean shorts and a matching blouse with nursery-rhyme figures on them. "Are you going now? Will you come back?" Delia asked me.

I hunkered down to her level. "Yes," I said. "But I'll come back to see you soon. I promise."

As I stood up I saw Mom and Dad watching me. "That's *all* I promise," I told them.

We left the Barker Home for Children and drove back to Metairie in silence. I guessed we all had too much to think about. I kept picturing Jimmy, with his lopsided grin, and the loving way Demetria looked at her little sister, and I discovered that I really wanted them to come and live with Mom and Dad and me at Graymoss.

Just then Mom said, "I'm exhausted. I suppose it was all the conflict this morning."

"Lie down for a while when we get home," Dad said. "I'll make dinner."

"I'll be all right," Mom said. "A nap will help. We'll be up awfully late tonight."

I bolted upright in shock as I realized what Mom meant. "Mom!" I cried out. "You can't go to Graymoss tonight."

Mom twisted around to look at me. "All day long you've been after me to spend the night at Graymoss to prove to everyone that the house is not haunted. Now that I've agreed, you don't want me to go. Why this sudden change of mind?"

I didn't know what to say. I couldn't tell her that the evil would surround her and terrify her, making her realize she couldn't create a home out of Graymoss. What would happen to Demetria and Delia and Robbie and Jimmy?

Ava Phipps had told me to find the cause of the

hauntings so that I could set the evil free. I'd try my best, but I had to have time.

I took a deep breath, looked right into Mom's eyes, and said, "I was wrong. You don't have to prove there are no ghosts to Mrs. Lord or Mr. Merle or anybody else in Bogue City. It's *your* house, not theirs. I don't think you should give in to them, Mom."

"Lia has a good point," Dad said.

Good old Dad. I was counting on him to back me up. He'd gladly drive Mom back to Graymoss if she wanted him to, but I was sure he was tired enough to want to skip another three- or four-hour round trip.

Mom turned around and settled back. "You're right, Lia," she said to me, although I could tell she was thinking things out loud to herself. "I don't have to prove anything to anybody. Besides, I'm tired and hungry and my feet hurt."

She laughed, and Dad laughed along with her.

But I didn't laugh. I'd just given myself the job of getting rid of whoever was haunting Graymoss, and I didn't know how I was going to do it.

# CHAPTER THIRTEEN

When we got home there were three messages from Grandma telling us that she'd returned to Baton Rouge earlier than she'd planned. She asked us to call her.

"After we've had something to eat," Mom said. She went into the kitchen to help Dad make dinner, and I dashed upstairs to telephone Jolie. I laid *Favorite Tales of Edgar Allan Poe* next to me on the bed.

Jolie squeaked and gasped while I told her everything that had happened. I finally said, "That's it. What should I do?"

"Call him," Jolie said. "He told you to, and you said he was a hunk, so call him."

Exasperated, I flopped back on the bed. "Jolie! I told you all about the people we met and what they said about the evil in Graymoss, and I told you about the kids and how I changed my mind, even though I didn't want to, and all you can tell me is 'Call him'?"

There was silence for a minute. Then Jolie said, "What do you expect me to say? We've been best friends forever, Lia, and now you want to move away. We'll never see each other."

"It's only a little over two hours' drive," I said. "We can get together often. You can come and spend the night."

"No thanks!" she said quickly.

"It'll be all right after the ghosts have left." I propped myself up on one elbow and said, "Oh, Jolie, moving away from you will be the hardest thing I've ever done in my life, but if you could see those kids who'll probably grow up without families . . ."

"Don't tell me any more about them," Jolie said. "Right now I don't want to hear because I'm not through feeling hurt and unhappy and a little bit mad."

"I'm sorry," I said.

"Don't be. It's not really your fault. Parents rule the world, and you would have moved to Graymoss whether you wanted to or not."

"Only if we could get rid of the evil."

The smell of onions and bell peppers frying wafted under my door and tickled my nose. My stomach rumbled, but I kept my mind on trying to solve the problem. "Mrs. Phipps didn't think the evil came from the grandfather," I said. "Nobody thinks so. He was a good guy, and this ghost is just plain nasty and evil."

"Maybe it's the ghost of one of those people

who stayed in the house at night and died of fright."

"No," I said. "Charlotte felt the evil. Remember? It happened the night her grandfather died."

"Wait a minute," Jolie told me. "I'm getting an idea."

Just then Mom called me. "Hurry up, Jolie," I said. "I've got to go."

"Okay," Jolie said. "Get Charlotte's diary and go over it carefully. Write down every single thing she said about her grandfather and every single thing he said. Take a good look at it. There might be a clue."

I got an idea of my own and added, "Or in what he didn't say?"

"Both. Want me to come over and help you?"

"Sure," I told her, beginning to feel hopeful for the first time. "After dinner. Okay?"

I ran down the stairs and into the kitchen. As I dropped into my chair at the table I said, "Mom, Jolie's coming over tonight."

"That's nice," Mom said.

Dad placed a bowl of rice and a bowl of shrimp stir-fry on the table.

"So would you give me Charlotte's diary? We want to read it again, together."

"Not on your life," Mom answered. "I locked up that diary and put it away forever. You read it twice, and that was two times too many. If you read it again, both you and Jolie will have nightmares for a month. Forget the diary. Forget the so-called ghosts. Ghosts don't exist."

I knew, from the expression on Mom's face, that

it wouldn't do any good to argue. I ate dinner, not even thinking about what I was tasting, and tried to figure out what to do next.

When Jolie came, she immediately made for the *Favorite Tales of Edgar Allan Poe*, which lay on my bed. "Wow!" she said as she carefully picked up the small book and ran a finger over the corner that had been burned. "This was Charlotte's."

"I've been looking through the stories," I explained, "trying to find a message."

Jolie held the book up and gently shook it. She carefully pried up the loose endpapers and looked under them. "Nothing here," she said. She put down the book and glanced around. "Where's Charlotte's diary?"

"Out of bounds. Mom's got some weird idea that we'll have nightmares."

"But we have to see the diary again," Jolie said. "It's not like you can just get a copy at the library."

I had picked up the book of Poe's stories, but now I nearly dropped it. "There *is* a copy of what Charlotte wrote," I said. "It's on display in the Bogue City Historical Society's museum."

For a moment Jolie brightened, but then she made a face. "That's a big help. How are you going to get to Bogue City to read it without your mom finding out?"

"I could visit Grandma in Baton Rouge," I said. With a grin I pulled Jonathan's father's card out of the pocket of my shirt and waved it at Jolie.

"Then I'll call Jonathan. He said he'd do anything he could to help me, and he's old enough to drive."

Jolie didn't grin in return. She frowned. "Just don't forget your gris-gris," she warned. "When you get around that house, anything might happen. Look what you saw already."

"Don't try to scare me," I said. "You're supposed to be helping me get rid of a ghost."

"Okay," Jolie said. "Fill me in. What have you found out by reading the Poe stories?"

"That there are ten short stories in this book, but because of Poe's writing style, with long paragraphs and lots of description, they're hard to skim. I'm going to be up late trying to finish reading them."

"Remember reading 'The Masque of the Red Death' last year in American lit?" Jolie asked. "It gave me shivers."

I nodded. "Mrs. Weems said that most of Poe's stories have some kind of surprise ending. They'd give anybody shivers."

"You'll have to read every one of the stories in Charlotte's book," Jolie said.

"I've already decided that," I told her. "I thought if I could compare the plots I might see which story Placide Blevins had in mind as a message."

"I'll help you," Jolie said. "Read off the names of the stories, and I'll write them down. Tell me the plot of each story, but keep it short, like one sentence."

I opened the book. "Let's see. Where should I start?"

"I wish Charlotte hadn't lost that bookmark," Jolie said.

"I do, too, but it's too late for wishing." I turned to the title page. " 'The Gold Bug,' 'The Murders in the Rue Morgue,' 'The Oval Portrait,' 'The Black Cat,' 'The Purloined Letter,' 'The Tell-Tale Heart,' 'The Fall of the House of Usher,' 'The Masque of the Red Death,' 'The Cask of Amontillado,' and 'The Pit and the Pendulum.' "

Jolie looked at the list. "Maybe the first letters of each word spell out a message."

"Forget it. That's a dumb old code we used in third grade. Are you ready to write?" I asked. "We can list the stories we've already read."

" 'The Masque of the Red Death,' " Jolie began. "Selfish prince hides in his castle with his friends to escape the plague that is killing everyone in his country, only at a ball the Red Death comes and kills the prince and his friends, too."

I made a face. "How long are these sentences supposed to be?"

Jolie waited until she had finished writing. "Very funny. You try it with the next one."

" 'The Murders in the Rue Morgue,' " I said. "Here goes. Neighbors hear screams and break into a locked room to find a woman missing and her murdered daughter stuffed up a chimney. A detective named C. Auguste Dupin—"

"That's more than one sentence," Jolie said.

"There was more than one murder. They found the woman's body in the courtyard."

"That doesn't matter. We agreed, one sentence."

"All right. After 'stuffed up a chimney,' write,

'so a detective is called in who solves the crime by finding a broken nail that proves the murderer left the room through a window and he wasn't a raving maniac because he—' "

"Stop," Jolie said. "This is getting too long."

"I don't see how it fits anything at Graymoss anyway," I told her.

"Don't try to figure it out now. Let's just write the sentences. Later on we can study them and see if anything fits. Next story."

" 'The Cask of Amontillado,' " I said. "I hated that story." I took a deep breath and thought hard. "A man gets revenge on an acquaintance who insulted him by luring him to his wine cellar and walling him up inside it."

Jolie finished writing and said, "Don't forget 'The Gold Bug.' A man is invited to help a friend find the location of Captain Kidd's buried treasure by dropping a gold bug through the eye of a skull nailed to a tree."

"Okay. Write it," I said. When she had finished I asked, "Any others?"

"No," she said. "How about you?"

I shook my head. "I have to read the rest of them."

"Then start reading," Jolie said.

I picked one of the shortest stories to read: "The Oval Portrait." It was only three pages so it didn't take long. I rested the book on my lap and said, "A wounded man and his valet break into an empty chateau to spend the night, and there's an oval portrait of a beautiful woman hanging on the wall, and the man reads what the woman's husband wrote, that he was an artist who ignored her for his art, and his neglect killed her."

"That's it?" Jolie asked.

When I nodded, she made a face of disgust, but wrote it anyway.

I felt a little guilty at my disloyalty to Charlotte, who had written in her diary that she enjoyed the stories, because Jolie and I didn't.

I was halfway through "The Tell-Tale Heart" when Jolie's mom called her to come home.

I took the notepad from her and said, "I'll finish the stories tonight."

"Let me know what you find out," Jolie said. She hesitated at the door. "About your visit to your grandma's—I hope you can go, but . . ." She suddenly hugged me. "Be awfully careful, Lia!"

After Jolie left I went looking for Mom and found her in the den. "Did you talk to Grandma?" I asked.

"Yes," Mom answered.

"Is she all right? I mean, you know. When her mother died that's the only time I've ever seen Grandma cry."

"She's all right. She just needs a little moral support," Mom said. She gave me a careful look. "Lia, I know you're enjoying your summer vacation with Jolie, but would you consider visiting your grandmother for a few days? We could drive you there tomorrow, and pick you up on Friday, when we meet the structural engineers at Graymoss."

I realized my mouth was open. I couldn't have

planned this any better. From Sunday to Friday I'd have almost five whole days to try to find the secret keeping the evil at Graymoss.

"I know sometimes you feel Grandma is a little hard to get along with," Mom said, "so if you don't want to visit her, I'll understand."

Mom was watching, waiting for my answer, so I quickly pulled my thoughts together and assured her, "I'd like to visit Grandma. I really would."

Mom smiled and reached for the telephone. "Thanks, honey," she said. "Grandma may not say so, but she'll be glad you're there, too. I'll give her a call."

I shot back up the stairs. Pack and read . . . don't forget the gris-gris . . . Read and pack. I had things to do.

I filled my canvas bag with shorts and T-shirts and tucked in a waist pack with a small flashlight inside. I even added one dress—just in case Grandma decided she wanted to go to a restaurant. I wasn't going to let myself in for another "young people nowdays don't have the slightest idea of how to dress properly" lectures.

Down in the bottom of the bag, I hid the bag of gris-gris. I felt a strange, prickly feeling as I remembered Ava Phipps wondering how long the gris-gris's power would work. Long enough, I hoped.

When I'd finished packing I returned to Poe's stories. I made good time through the rest of "The Tell-Tale Heart," and wrote,

A madman murders and dismembers an old man because he doesn't like one of his eyes, but

144

he keeps thinking he hears the old man's heart beating under the floorboards of his bedroom so he confesses to the police.

*How is any of this horror stuff going to help me understand the evil in Graymoss?* I wondered. But I realized that the evil was a horror in itself, so maybe there was a connection I hadn't discovered yet.

Mom tapped at my door and called, "Good night, Lia. Don't stay up reading too late." That was what she always said.

"I won't," I called back. That was what I always answered.

In a few moments the house was silent, and I kept reading and writing one-sentence plots. A little after midnight I finished—thank goodness. I read over what I'd just written.

"The Purloined Letter"—Auguste Dupin discovers the hiding place of a stolen letter and brings about the political downfall of the thief.

"The Black Cat"—a man tortures and kills his cat, then makes a home for another cat, which is really the spirit of the first cat, but before he can go down in the basement to kill the cat again, the man's wife intervenes so he murders her, but the cat gets its revenge and the man is caught by the police.

The sentence was too long, but I shrugged. A lot went on in that horror story.

"The Pit and the Pendulum"—A man in Toledo, Spain, is tortured in a gruesome prison cell but just before he gives in to death he is rescued by the French army.

"The Fall of the House of Usher"—The narrator visits a friend, Roderick Usher, who lives in a gloomy old house, and while he is there Usher's sister Madeline dies and is put into a locked coffin in a basement vault, but at night all sorts of horrible noises are heard and scary things happen until finally Madeline, who wasn't dead after all, breaks out of her coffin and appears to Roderick, who dies just before the house is torn apart by a whirlwind.

I stopped writing and studied that extra-long sentence. Jolie would have had something to say about that, but I couldn't help it. I sat thinking about the story, which made me uncomfortable. There were so many scary descriptions of sounds and winds and footsteps and unearthly things, it reminded me of Graymoss at night.

I carefully went over the story descriptions, one by one, seeing if any of the others applied in even the smallest way to Graymoss.

I crossed out "The Gold Bug," since there was no pirate treasure in Graymoss. "The Oval Portrait" didn't fit because I hadn't seen a portrait of anybody at all at Graymoss and Charlotte hadn't mentioned one. "The Black Cat" didn't help, because there had been no mention of the Blevinses owning a cat, so I crossed it out, too, along with "The Pit and the Pendulum" and "The Purloined Letter." I didn't see how "The Tell-Tale Heart" would fit, or "The Masque of the Red Death." They took place inside houses, but that was the only link.

That left "The Murders in the Rue Morgue," "The Cask of Amontillado," and "The Fall of the House of Usher."

I waited for inspiration to strike, but it didn't. My eyes hurt, my fingers ached, and I couldn't stop yawning.

Disappointed that I hadn't found some important key that would solve the problem, I put down the book, turned out the light, and slid down in bed, ready to sleep.

Only I didn't sleep. Charlotte's grandfather had tried to give her a message through Poe's stories. She didn't know what the message was, and neither did I. My mind was a jumble of hideous corpses who'd been throttled, and screaming cats that had been knifed, and locked doors that were thrown open, and bricked-up walls, and detached hearts that kept beating. How could any of this lead to the truth about Graymoss? Which story held the clue?

# CHAPTER FOURTEEN

We arrived at Grandma's house at noon, just in time for dinner. Grandma had always followed the old custom of a big Sunday dinner at midday with a supper of leftovers in the evening. She did herself proud with a huge pot roast simmered with red potatoes, carrots, celery, and onions. There were two kinds of salads and beaten biscuits.

I had dumped my bag on the middle of the bed in her guest room, and I sat quietly eating and listening as she went over and over proud memories of her mother.

When we had finished a dessert of homemade lemon ice cream, Grandma gave Mom and me each a small box. "Mother wasn't interested in jewelry, so she didn't own much," she said. "However, I'd like the two of you to enjoy the pieces that meant the most to her."

Mom opened her box and exclaimed with delight over a delicate gold pin and ring set with amethysts. My gift was a pair of small pearl stud earrings, which I loved. I put them on and thanked Grandma.

"When you wear them I hope you'll remember your great-grandmother as an outstanding role model. Sarah Langley was a courageous woman who was not afraid to tackle problems and conquer them," Grandma said to me. In my mind the banner with the embroidered names of Women Who Are Exceptionally Brave appeared in full color over Grandma's head.

I hoped she wouldn't start in on how I wasn't like a single one of the women in the family, so quiet and shy with my nose always in a book.

I braced myself, just in case, but Mom suddenly pushed back her chair and began clearing the table. "Derek and I have to get back," she said. "I've got a stack of paperwork to finish before I return to work tomorrow. In fact, I may just stop off at the office and see how much work has piled up while I was in California."

Grandma looked disappointed. "About Graymoss—I had hoped to hear about your visit there," she began, and I realized that was really what she wanted to talk about.

"There's really nothing to tell," Mom said. Before she disappeared into the kitchen with a stack of plates, she added, "We've hired an engineering firm to check out the structure on Friday. We won't know what we'll be doing with the house until then."

"On her deathbed Mother warned Lia that—"

Mom wasn't about to let Grandma finish what she had to say about Graymoss. Somehow I found myself volunteering to put the dishes in the dishwasher so that Mom and Dad could leave.

"See you on Friday, honey," Mom said. She and Dad kissed me goodbye and left.

Grandma didn't come back to the kitchen until I had almost finished. She leaned against the sink and fixed me with such a steady gaze that I felt like a bug on a slide in science class. "You were with your parents when they visited Graymoss, weren't you, Lia?"

"Yes," I answered.

"Tell me what you found there. Tell me everything."

I don't know where I got the sudden burst of courage. Maybe it came from wearing the remarkable Sarah Langley's earrings. Maybe it was just because I was so eager to find out everything I could about Graymoss. I stared directly back into Grandma's eyes and said, "I'll tell, if you will."

"What?" Grandma looked amazed.

I took a deep breath and said, "You wouldn't tell Mom and me everything that happened to you at Graymoss, and I want to know, so I'll tell you what happened to me if you tell me what happened to you."

Grandma examined me as though I were someone she hadn't met before. I could tell she was thinking hard. "Very well," she said. "You first."

I was on a roll and enjoying my sudden burst of

power. "No, Grandma," I said. "You first. I asked you *my* question back when we were in San Francisco."

Grandma sighed. "I guess that's fair," she said, and handed me a towel to dry my hands. "Let's go into the living room, where we can be comfortable."

The telephone interrupted us.

Grandma picked up the kitchen extension. As she listened, worry wrinkles spread across her forehead and around her eyes. "Yes," she said, and then, "Oh, dear. No, you won't be able to reach them for the next few hours. Yes, I'll come."

My chest hurt, and I found it hard to breathe. As Grandma hung up the receiver I blurted out, "Mom and Dad are all right, aren't they? What happened?"

"They're fine. That call wasn't about your parents," Grandma said, but the worry lines didn't go away.

"Then what's the matter? Who called you?"

I could see Grandma making an effort to pull herself together. "It was a sheriff in Bogue Parish," she said. "According to the sheriff, Charlie Boudreau went to Graymoss this afternoon and discovered that the summer kitchen had completely collapsed."

I let out a sigh of relief. "That's no big deal," I said. "Dad was planning to tear it down anyway."

"Please allow me to finish," Grandma said sternly. "Charlie noticed a leg sticking out of all that rubble, so he pulled away the boards as fast as he could. Lying there was a man named Raymond Merle."

I gasped. "He was dead?"

"No. He's alive but unconscious. Fortunately, the doctors in the hospital here in Baton Rouge, where the ambulance took him, told the sheriff it was more than likely Mr. Merle would pull through." She paused. "The sheriff couldn't reach your parents, as the owners of the property, so I told him I'd meet him at Graymoss and give him whatever information he needs."

"I'm going, too," I told Grandma.

I expected her to argue, but she looked relieved. "We can compare stories on the ride," she said. "My story doesn't take long to tell."

"Neither does mine," I said. "Wait for me. I'll be right back."

I tore upstairs to get my gris-gris, but I stopped short, gasping, as I saw that my canvas bag was gone. I ran back to the top of the stairs and yelled, "Grandma! What happened to my things?"

She appeared below me. "I don't hold with living out of suitcases and leaving clothes draped all over chairs and the floor, the way you did the last time you were here, so I unpacked for you and put your clothes in the emptied dresser drawers. The dress is on a hanger in the closet."

A chill trickled from the back of my neck all the way down to my toes. "Where's my bag?" I asked. "Where did you put it?"

"On the floor of the closet." She sighed. "Lia, I know voodoo symbols when I see them. They're totally meaningless in themselves, but they can cause great damage to those who believe in them. People have actually taken to their beds and died because enemies have left voodoo charms of death at their doors."

"My gris-gris isn't bad voodoo," I explained. "The woman who sold it to me said it would protect me from the evil in Graymoss."

"Nonsense. Voodoo won't protect you against anything," Grandma said.

"But it will!" I shouted. "When we were in the house and I held on to the gris-gris, nothing happened. But when I let go of it I saw the invisible body on the bed!"

Grandma paled. She reached out and clutched the knob on the foot of the stair railing. She wavered for a moment, as though she were trying to steady herself. Finally she gulped and said, "Forget the voodoo, Lia. I told the sheriff's deputy we'd come right away. Let's go."

I backed away from the railing and tried to think. Grandma hadn't gone out to the garage, where she kept her trash can, so she'd probably thrown the gris-gris in her own wastepaper basket. I fastened my waist pack, rummaged through the basket, and found the gris-gris at the bottom, wrapped in a tissue. With her X-ray eyes Grandma would probably spot the gris-gris if I wore it under my shirt, so I dropped it into my waist pack next to my flashlight.

A few minutes later we were on the road into Bogue City. Grandma said, "Years ago, when your grandfather and I moved to Baton Rouge, Mother asked me to keep an occasional eye on Graymoss. I would have done so. I had every intention of fulfilling her request, but . . ."

"What did you see when you were in the house?" I asked.

"I had been conversing with Charlie Boudreau when a storm came up," she said. "Charlie hurried to his truck and drove home, but I didn't want to drive back to Baton Rouge in a downpour, so I decided to wait out the storm inside the house." She paused. "In spite of Charlie's warning."

"What did he say?" I asked.

"He told me to remember what was written in Charlotte's diary and said he wouldn't be caught dead at Graymoss after dark."

Grandma didn't speak for a few moments, and I realized I had been holding my breath, so I let it out in a whoosh.

"But you stayed there anyway? And it got dark?"

"Yes. While I was there darkness fell." She shuddered and said, "I don't like to remember what happened. I can't bear to think about it."

"Tell me!" I cried out impatiently.

"I would if I could," Grandma said. "I don't really know. It seems there were sounds and whispered words and—"

"What words? What did the voices say?"

Grandma shook her head. "I didn't try to make the words out. I couldn't. I was standing by the window, watching the lightning flash, when I thought I felt something touch my cheek."

When she didn't go on, I asked, "And then what?"

Grandma cleared her throat, but it still sounded raspy. "And then I fainted," she said. "I came to and the storm had passed. I picked myself up off that dusty floor, ran outside as fast as I could, and drove away."

Grandma was strictly a keep-your-eyes-on-the-road kind of driver, so it surprised me when she turned to look at me. "You needn't repeat that part to your parents," she said. "Goodness knows, I was terribly embarrassed to tell my own mother I had been so frightened I had fainted, as if I didn't have a good, sensible brain in my head. But I did tell her. I had to tell her, because I thought of what a waste it was to keep up a house that no one could live in, just because an ancestor back in Civil War times had insisted on it."

"Great-grandmother Sarah said you wanted to destroy the house."

"I did indeed. I still do."

We pulled up to the gate on the drive leading to Graymoss. I didn't have to get out to open the gate because it was already open wide. Grandma drove down the road, and as we approached the house I saw a car from the sheriff's department parked next to Charlie's pickup truck.

A heavyset, graying man in uniform walked over and introduced himself as Sheriff Lee Fuller.

"How is Mr. Merle?" Grandma asked.

"Some better," Sheriff Fuller said. "He's conscious now, but with a bad headache."

"Did he tell you what happened?"

"They've got him doped up some for the pain. He broke an arm, too, by the way. He's not sayin' too much right now—just that somethin' pushed him."

"Do you mean *someone?*"

"Nope. Ray said *somethin'* pushed him. You

155

know how spooked everyone is about this place, especially at night."

"Ghosts don't push people," Grandma said.

"I've got some forms to fill out. You can help me with 'em," Sheriff Fuller said, and walked toward his car. In a low voice I said to Grandma, "What about Charlotte's cousin Lydia, who got pushed on the stairs?"

Grandma frowned. "Was that in the diary? I don't seem to remember it."

"A copy of the diary is in the historical museum here," I said, delighted that I had a good excuse to visit it. "Let's stop by and read what Charlotte said."

Sheriff Fuller returned with a clipboard and pen. "I need the full name and address of the rightful owner of this property, since Ray was on the property at the time the accident happened."

Grandma's eyes blazed. "He was *trespassing* on private property!" she snapped. "He had no business being here."

I suddenly realized what Sheriff Fuller had said earlier. "You told us Mr. Merle was here at night."

"That's right."

"Why?"

"That's one of the questions I'm fixin' to ask him, when he's able to answer," Sheriff Fuller said.

I was puzzled as to why Mr. Merle had come to Graymoss at night—and especially last night, after Mom and Dad had sent him away. If Mom *had* come back, as I had first wanted her to do, she would have been furious to have Mr. Merle as a late-night visitor.

As I glanced toward the house I felt uncomfortable, as though something about the house itself were tied in to Mr. Merle's accident and I needed to find out what it was. I hadn't a clue. I waited until Grandma had finished with the sheriff and then asked, "Have you looked inside the house?"

Sheriff Fuller looked surprised. "No need," he said. "The accident happened outside."

"Mr. Merle didn't belong here in the first place—especially at night," I said. "We should find out if he had been inside the house, too."

"Are you saying, in case he broke in?" Sheriff Fuller asked.

Grandma looked a little pale. "I don't see any need to go inside the house—" she began, but I interrupted.

"It's important," I said. "Mom and Dad would want us to. What if Mr. Merle gets any ideas about suing for injuries?"

Grandma looked a little nervous, but she was the one who had brought up trespassing, so she nodded agreement.

"I've never been inside the place," Sheriff Fuller said hesitantly. "I mean, I've heard . . . everybody's heard that . . ."

"If Mr. Merle does sue us, you may be called as a witness," I told him. "You'll be asked how you investigated the accident."

"I'll get the keys from Charlie," Sheriff Fuller said.

We all followed Charlie, who unlocked the front door but insisted on staying outside.

"Tell us about the people who died of fright at Graymoss," I said to the sheriff.

"Can't," he said. "I've heard the stories, but I've

157

never been able to find records or names. I figure that way back somebody got to swappin' stories about the house, got carried away, and made up a few stories of their own."

I nodded, satisfied. That narrowed down the number of ghosts I'd have to deal with.

Sheriff Fuller entered the house, but Grandma hung back. She was no longer able to hide her fear.

"You'll be all right. Wear this," I said quietly. I reached into my waist pack, pulled out the little bag of gris-gris, and hung it around her neck.

Grandma was too frightened to really notice what I was doing or object. Without my gris-gris for protection, I was pretty scared myself. I took Grandma's hand and pulled her over the threshold.

I was fairly sure that Mr. Merle wouldn't have had access to Charlie's keys. He would have found another way to get into the house. I wondered how many people knew about the broken window sash in the kitchen. As Grandma and Sheriff Fuller nervously tiptoed around the entry hall, looking like a couple of housebreakers themselves, I stopped and listened. The hair on the back of my neck rose as I thought I heard a faint cry. *It sounds like a cat,* I told myself. *It has to be one of Mrs. Phipps's cats.* I walked through the dining room and into the kitchen.

A tire iron lay on the floor next to the wide-open door to the basement. Wood had been splintered on the door frame around the lock.

"Grandma! Sheriff Fuller!" I shouted. "Come here! Quick!"

They dashed in behind me.

"I'll be darned. Looks like ol' Ray did some damage here," Sheriff Fuller said.

I stepped aside to get out of the way, and as I did I glanced down the stairs into the basement. A dim greenish light shone through the basement windows, casting a sickly glow on the body of a man who lay on his back at the foot of the cement stairs. His wide eyes stared straight up into mine.

# CHAPTER FIFTEEN

I hung on to Grandma and tried not to scream. A kind of whimpering, strangling sound came out.

"What's goin' on?" Sheriff Fuller asked. "What's the matter?"

The man at the foot of the stairs suddenly raised his head and yelled, "What took y'all so long? Didn't anybody hear me shouting?"

Grandma kept making gasping noises, and for a few moments my mind refused to work. Sheriff Fuller reacted faster. He trotted down the stairs and bent over the man. "Homer," he said. "What the hell happened to you?"

"That's Homer Tavey," I said to Grandma. "We met him yesterday. He's an antiques dealer and he's awfully pushy. He was really pressuring Mom."

Grandma recovered rapidly. She leaned into

the doorway and shouted down the stairs, "What are you doing breaking into our basement, Mr. Tavey?"

"Whoever you are, lady, don't you give me any grief," Mr. Tavey said. "My right leg's broke, and my back hurts somethin' awful. I'm in a lot of pain."

Sheriff Fuller took the steps two at a time. "I'm gonna radio in for an ambulance," he said to Grandma. "See if you can find a blanket or somethin' to put over him."

Grandma headed toward the parlor, but I carefully walked down the stairs. The railings were intact. The cement stairs weren't slippery. I reached Mr. Tavey and was about to sit next to him on the lower step when I saw a movement in the shadows. Two yellow eyes in a mound of black fur gleamed at me.

"The cat!" I cried, and took a step toward it.

The black cat gave a terrible cry. It shot out of its hiding place and disappeared into the depths of the cellar.

My legs shook as I clung to the railing, lowering myself to the steps. "How long has that cat been here?" I asked Mr. Tavey.

"You shouldn't have chased it off. Cats keep rats away."

"I didn't mean to chase it. I . . . Oh, never mind. How did you fall?"

"I don't know," he said. His lower lip protruded in a pout. "I was at the top of the stairs, and then suddenly I wasn't. It was like something pushed me."

"You mean *somebody*."

161

"I don't know what I mean. I was being quiet, so if there'd been footsteps I think I would have heard them."

"Ripping open a door with a tire iron isn't being very quiet," I pointed out.

Mr. Tavey groaned. "I know what it looks like—breaking and entering—except it wasn't, not really."

"It looks like you were going to steal something," I said.

He groaned again. "I just wanted to see the wine cellar. In that copy of a diary that Mrs. Lord is so blamed proud of there's something about a wine cellar. If there were any bottles left, can you imagine what a collector would pay for them?"

"To you?"

"To your folks," Mr. Tavey said. "Honest. I'd get a little something for arranging the deal, a nice percentage, but that would be all. Your folks wouldn't know their value. When they cleaned up the basement they'd probably toss the bottles out."

"Why didn't you just ask Mom and Dad if you could see the wine cellar?"

Mr. Tavey grimaced, squeezing his eyes shut. "Your mother didn't want to listen to anything I had to say."

"So you thought if you just found the wine and took it, nobody would miss it because they wouldn't have known it was there."

"Yes. I mean no. I mean . . ."

"You mean you are a scoundrel and a thief," Grandma said. She clumped down the stairs, squeezing past me, and covered Mr. Tavey with a heavy, yellowed linen tablecloth. Then she

162

slipped what looked like a small, folded kitchen towel under his head. I wondered if she had been afraid to go upstairs alone and that was why she took the first things handy.

I wasn't through questioning Mr. Tavey. This was the only chance I had, before the sheriff returned. "What time did you get here?" I asked.

"Right after Charlie left. It was before five o'clock. I wanted to leave here before your parents returned."

Mr. Tavey had been in the house all night! He could tell us better than anyone else what went on at Graymoss. But I was puzzled. If he'd experienced the voices and faces and all the other horrible things that had been reported, he should have been scared out of his mind.

"You were in the house at night," I said. "What did you see and hear? Tell me!"

"Nothing." He grimaced again and raised both hands, pressing his palms against the side of his head. "I was knocked out colder than a catfish. When I woke up the sun was up and I could hear y'all walking around."

I stepped back, disappointed, but suddenly one more question occurred to me. "Mr. Tavey," I asked, "what made you think my parents were coming back to Graymoss last night?"

His voice was filled with surprise. "Why, everybody knew that. Your mama thought she was gonna prove that Graymoss wasn't haunted."

*How could "everybody" know Mom's plans when she hadn't even made them yet?* I wondered.

I left Grandma to sit with Mr. Tavey. I pulled my flashlight out of my waist pack and walked through the basement, wary that I might suddenly come upon that fearsome cat. The basement wasn't very large, and there were twists and turns in it. Near the back the walls narrowed. There were shelves on my left. They were filled with some small tools and household clutter, like most basements, although I guessed that most of that clutter would be valuable now because it was so old. Some of the things on the shelf I couldn't recognize. There was something with jagged teeth—like a very small saw; a tapered, pointed metal bar; a flat, pointed piece of iron with a handle; and a low, rectangular pan half-filled with white stuff under a crust of dirt and dust. I did recognize a few garden tools and a wooden mallet.

One shelf held three very dusty bottles of what once had most likely been wine. I rubbed at one and could read part of its French label. Three bottles? Some wine cellar. Mr. Tavey had caused himself a lot of trouble for nothing.

On my right was a short brick wall that joined two concrete walls. It was plain, except in the middle, where the brick design formed a kind of arch. Farther on, at the very back of the basement, I could spot a window with most of the glass missing. The beam of my flashlight struck a jagged edge that had caught a clump of what looked like black fur, so I knew how that cat had entered and where it had gone. I retraced my route and joined Grandma and Mr. Tavey.

Grandma was lecturing him sternly about honesty and respecting other people's property. Mr. Tavey had a desperate look in his eyes.

The sheriff and paramedics appeared, and in a

short while Mr. Tavey was on his way to the hospital in Baton Rouge.

"Nothin' more I can do here," Sheriff Fuller told Grandma and me as we stepped out on the veranda. He carried Mr. Tavey's tire iron to hold for evidence. "I'm going on to the hospital to talk to Ray. You ladies will be all right, won't you?"

"We'll be fine," Grandma said.

We watched the sheriff stop to talk to Charlie before he drove off. Then we walked toward Grandma's car. "Will you lock up the house, please, Charlie?" Grandma asked.

Charlie shifted from one foot to the other. "I understand Homer Tavey done some damage to the basement door frame. You ain't gonna ask me to clean it up now, are you?"

"Why not?" Grandma asked. "Your job includes making repairs, doesn't it?"

"My wife, May, will be here to clean come Monday next," he said. "I'd just as soon wait for her. I make it a policy not to set foot in that house if I can help it, and never when I'm gonna be alone in it."

"Suit yourself." Grandma shrugged. "As long as the repairs get done."

Charlie tilted his head as he looked at me. "Why didn't your parents come back here last night, like they was goin' to?"

"Why did you think they were going to?" I asked.

He looked surprised. "They was gonna stay in the house so your mother could prove it wasn't haunted. Everybody knew that."

As we climbed into the car and drove toward

Bogue City I said, "Small-town news is faster than e-mail!"

Grandma nodded. "Somebody starts a piece of information and it goes right through town."

"But it was wrong information."

"Lots of rumors get started in small towns, too," Grandma said, "but let's not waste time discussing trivia. We have something to talk about. For your own good I threw away your voodoo charm. I don't appreciate your sneaking it back."

"I didn't sneak it. I took it because it's mine," I told her. "It's gris-gris, and it protects against ghosts."

"It's foolishness," she said.

"You didn't think so when I hung it around your neck." I took a good look at Grandma, but I didn't see the string or the little bag. "Where is it, Grandma? What did you do with it?"

Grandma blushed. "I didn't want to enter that house. I freely admit it. Perhaps I was more nervous than I should have been because I didn't realize what you were doing when you gave me the gris-gris, as you call it. I first discovered I was wearing it when I was tending to Mr. Tavey."

I held out a hand. "Will you give it back to me?"

"You don't need it," she said. "Besides, I no longer have it."

I shuddered. I was counting on that gris-gris for what I needed to do. "Where is it?" I asked.

"Somewhere in the basement," she answered. "When I realized what I was wearing, I pulled it off and threw it as far as I could."

"Oh, Grandma," I moaned. "It was *mine*. I need it."

"No, you don't," Grandma said. "My job is to take care of you while you're visiting me, so I feel totally justified in my actions."

I probably would have kept arguing, but we were on the main street of Bogue City, and there was something else I had to do. "Stop the car, Grandma. Please!" I said. "See that sign? There's the historical museum. If it's open we can take another look at what Charlotte wrote in her diary."

Grandma probably didn't want to squelch me a second time, so she parked her car, and we went to the door. An Open sign hung over the glass, and inside I could see a woman with blue-white hair seated at a table.

As soon as we were inside the museum, Grandma signed the register and paid an entry fee. While the woman at the table trilled on and on to Grandma about the glorious future of Graymoss— if only it were to belong to the historical society— I glanced around the one small room.

There were lots of framed photographs of people from long ago. There were even two photos of Graymoss, along with a large painting of the house that wasn't very good. On the back wall hung some farming tools from the 1800s and somebody had made an illustrated chart of local wildflowers. Two mannequins were dressed in old-fashioned clothing, and on a shelf behind them rested a row of high-buttoned shoes.

There were a number of other things on exhibit

in the museum, but I saw what I had come to examine and hurried toward it. Along one wall was a row of posterboards with sections from Charlotte's diary copied on them.

I reached into my waist pack and pulled out a small notepad and a pen. As fast as I could I copied everything Charlotte had written about Placide Blevins. I didn't stop to think about what I wrote. I just needed to get it all down on paper.

I had finished and was shoving the notebook back into my waist pack when a hand rested on my shoulder.

"I'm almost through, Grandma," I said.

"I'm not your Grandma," a deep voice said.

Jonathan laughed as I whirled around.

"I didn't expect to see you here," I told him.

"You said you'd call me if you came back. I thought you might call last night."

"I didn't know I'd be here today. The sheriff called Grandma and asked her to come. Do you know about Mr. Merle?"

"Yes," Jonathan said. "Ray Merle should have known better. That's what comes of playing Halloween in the dark."

I took a step back and studied him. "What do you mean, 'playing Halloween'?"

"Figure it out. Merle really wants to make a deal for that property. He was probably hiding near the house, waiting for your parents to show up. If the ghosts didn't do their job of scaring them out of their minds, he would have filled in. He just picked the wrong place to hide."

"Did he tell the sheriff that?"

"As far as I know, he hasn't told the sheriff anything. It's just something we all know."

"I supposed you know about Mr. Tavey, too."

Jonathan nodded. "News travels fast around here."

I suddenly remembered something. "I only told one person that Mom might be at Graymoss last night," I said. "And that was *you.*"

Jonathan didn't look apologetic or even embarrassed. He even chuckled as he answered, "I only told one person—my grandmother. If she passed it on, it's not my fault."

"It was private information, just between you and me."

"You didn't say so, Lia. That's not my fault, either."

He was right. I hadn't asked him not to tell. I had just assumed that he wouldn't.

"Don't be mad at me," Jonathan said. "I can't ask you to go out with me if you're mad."

"I'm not mad," I said. *Mad* wasn't the word for what I felt. *Disappointed,* maybe, or . . . I perked up. Was Jonathan asking me for a date?

"You're here with your grandmother. Does that mean you aren't going back to Metairie today? Will you be staying with her in Baton Rouge?" Jonathan asked.

I couldn't believe it. "Do you know everything about my family?"

"Just the facts I can put together," he said. "But I'd like to know more about *you.* Some of the kids around here are getting together at Ronnie Trudeau's house tonight. We're going to eat pizza and play CDs and dance. It's casual, jeans or shorts. Want to come with me?"

"Sure, but I'll have to ask Grandma."

For a moment I closed my eyes and wished I were someplace—anyplace—far, far away. I had done it again—said what a five-year-old would say.

Grandma had been moving closer and closer as she read the copy of Charlotte's diary. She stepped up and questioned, "What do you have to ask me?"

Bumbling and blushing, I managed to introduce Jonathan.

He told Grandma about the party, smoothly working in that his grandmother was Hannah Lord, the president of the Historical Society; that Ronnie Trudeau's father was president of the Bogue City bank; and that both Mr. and Mrs. Trudeau would be on hand to chaperone the party.

Grandma melted at Jonathan's charm. She gave him directions to her house, and he said he'd pick me up at seven.

On our drive back to Baton Rouge, Grandma said, "There's something different about you, Lia. You aren't such a quiet, timid little thing. I'm delighted that you seem to be . . . well, blossoming."

I did my best to keep a straight face as she went on. "And I'm glad you are now more interested in socializing. Jonathan seems like a nice boy. He has lovely manners."

*Agreed*, I thought, *but he's got a big mouth. I'm afraid to trust him.*

"He's very poised and polished for his age."

*Maybe so smoothly*, I thought, *that he's slippery.*

"And he's quite good-looking." Her eyes crinkled, and she smiled, as though we were girlfriends.

"Right," I said.

"I hope you have a lovely time at the party," Grandma said.

"Thank you." I leaned back against the seat and smiled, totally satisfied at the way my life was going. I didn't care about the party. I was pretty sure I wasn't ever going to care very much about Jonathan. But I did care about getting into Graymoss after dark—with or without the gris-gris. Jonathan didn't know it yet, but he was going to take me there.

# CHAPTER SIXTEEN

I took a quick shower and put on jeans and a pink cotton knit shirt. I had two hours to study my notes and look for a possible tie-in with one of Edgar Allan Poe's stories.

I began to read and underline, and it was tough going. All I knew about Placide Blevins was that he was good and kind and wasn't afraid of hard work. He had even helped to build Graymoss, and he'd constructed an herb garden for Charlotte. However, since he had grown older and no longer had the help of his son, he'd had to hire someone else—Morgan Slade.

Mr. Blevins liked to live well and eat well, and he enjoyed French wine. I smiled as I thought of his so-called fine wine cellar, comparing those three pitiful bottles to the huge racks that lined the walls in some of the best restaurants in New Orleans.

He was a brave, courageous man, though. He fought to protect Charlotte from Slade.

I read over what he had said about the valuables Slade was stealing: *They are of no real importance.* What he obviously meant, but hadn't said, was, "In comparison to your safety, Charlotte." I liked Mr. Blevins's priorities. I read again that Charlotte was told that the answers to her questions could be found in the pages of Poe's *Tales*. And I studied Charlotte's statement that her grandfather had told her to save the house.

Surprised, I spoke aloud. "No, he didn't, Charlotte. You said that he whispered, 'The house.' That's all."

Charlotte had thought she knew what he'd wanted to say and had finished the sentence for him, but what if he really wanted to say something else? What was it? Something *about* the house? Something *inside* the house?

A bad feeling about Morgan Slade bothered me, too. Something about him was said . . . or wasn't said. What was it? At the moment I couldn't put my finger on it.

I opened my notebook to the pages with the one-sentence descriptions of the *Favorite Tales*. I crossed out "The Murders in the Rue Morgue." Nobody in the Blevins household had been murdered and stuffed up a chimney, like the girl in that story. "The Murders in the Rue Morgue" was also what our American lit teacher called "a locked-room mystery," where the victim is in a locked room and the detective has to try to prove how someone else got in and murdered him and got out again. The story just didn't fit.

After a lot of thought I returned the story "The Black Cat" to my list. I realized that the Blevinses didn't have a black cat, but they did have a basement, and in the story the man murders his wife on the basement stairs. If Mr. Tavey had been pushed, as he claimed, his fall could have ended up as a murder, instead of just a broken leg. And with the black cat sitting there, watching . . . There was so much coincidence I had to keep considering the story for possible clues.

There was also a basement in "The Cask of Amontillado." That was the location of the wine cellar.

"The Fall of the House of Usher" had a sealed casket instead of a wine cellar, and, again, there was a basement. This story also described a lot of the same type of strange winds and noises that had terrified Charlotte. I wondered if she hadn't seen the similarity, too. Maybe she was too frightened to think about it clearly.

*And how about you?* I asked myself. *Are you thinking clearly? You're getting ready to go into a house that is haunted by evil, and you have nothing to protect you, now that you've lost the gris-gris.*

I glanced into the mirror over the dresser, but I didn't see my own reflection. Instead I could see Demetria and Jimmy and Delia looking back at me. I *had* to find the answer Charlotte couldn't find. I *had* to confront the evil in the house and send it away. I *had* to.

Suddenly words in the diary began to stand out.

Things Mr. Blevins said and didn't say shifted, shimmered, and took shape like puzzle pieces sliding together in my mind. I clutched the edge of the dresser, held my breath, and let it all happen. I was so scared that I shook. I knew now what I had to do. And I wasn't going to like it.

The doorbell rang, and I jumped. With trembling fingers, I closed my notebook and stuffed it into my waist pack, made sure my flashlight was working, and zipped the pack shut before I hurried down the stairs to meet Jonathan.

Before we left I asked Grandma if I could borrow her cell phone. "Dad says when anyone's out on the highway, especially at night—"

"He's right," Grandma said. She took the phone off its charger and handed it to me. It was small enough to stuff into my waist pack.

All the way out of Baton Rouge Jonathan talked about the party, and who would be there, and who was dating whom, and a lot of stuff I really didn't care about. My mind was on Graymoss and what I needed to do.

When Jonathan finally began to wind down I said, "I don't want to go to the party."

He whirled toward me. "What?"

"If it's all right with you, I'd rather go to Graymoss."

"You're kidding. Right?"

"No, I mean it. I hope you'll take me to Graymoss."

Jonathan threw me a couple of you've-got-to-be-crazy looks before he began thinking about what I'd said.

"It'll be dark soon. Real soon."

"That's what I'm counting on."

"I think I see what you mean. Nobody will be there," he said. "Nobody but you, me, and the ghosts." He actually leered.

"Don't get the wrong idea," I said. "I need to go to Graymoss, and you're the logical one to take me there."

"Sure," he said. "And if the ghosts don't show up, you and I will have the place to ourselves."

"I'm counting on the ghosts showing up," I told him.

"What ghosts?"

"What do you mean, 'what ghosts?' You felt them yourself. You told us so."

Jonathan threw back his head and laughed. "That story I told your mom about sneaking into the house when I was ten? Grandma got me to do that to help her cause. It came right out of that diary Grandma has plastered all over her museum. Sure, I climbed in that broken window and explored the house, but I did it as a dare when I was a kid, and it was in daylight. Charlie came around the corner and saw a bunch of us hanging around and chased us away."

I was stunned. "What you told us wasn't true?"

Jonathan looked smug. "No, but it made a good story for people who believe in ghosts."

"You're telling me that you don't believe in ghosts?"

"Of course I don't," he said, "and neither do you. Your story was pretty good, too. I have to admit you threw me a curve about that book falling and hitting you. I thought at first that you

176

were making fun of my story because the book-throwing was my own, original touch."

"My story was true," I said.

He stopped grinning and gave me another searching look.

"I can't figure you out," he said. "What do you want?"

"I told you. I want to go to Graymoss."

For a moment I wondered if Jonathan's presence would hurt my plan to get rid of the evil that haunted Graymoss, but I realized that Jonathan meant nothing to the evil. The only problem might be Jonathan's, if he fell under the full fury of the evil and got scared out of his skull.

We had reached Bogue City. I didn't have much time to convince Jonathan to take me there. He wouldn't believe the truth, so I appealed to his big ego. I said, "Look, it's a dare. Okay? A friend expects me to stay in the house until midnight, and I hoped you'd like to be with me."

Jonathan understood that. He smiled, and his car picked up speed. "We'll be there in five minutes," he said.

The gate was closed, but not locked, so I pushed it open, and we drove up to the house. Jonathan smiled again, and this time I smiled in return. If everything went as I thought it would, he'd be in for a huge surprise.

The sunset was a red and gold glow that spread from the horizon to tint the house, so the entire building seemed to gleam, and its western windows reflected flashes of fire. Even Jonathan seemed impressed.

We went up the back steps and walked as quietly as we could along the veranda to the window with the broken sash. As we reached it, the sun dropped behind the trees, and the glow vanished as suddenly as if a switch had been pulled.

We climbed in through the window. I handed Jonathan the flashlight he'd brought in from the car and took mine out of my pack. The light in the house was fading into purple and blue shadows, but we didn't need our flashlights yet.

The basement door was no longer open, although the broken splinters and scraps of wood still lay on the floor. I wondered who had shut the door. Charlie had insisted he wouldn't set foot inside the house. Had the sheriff shut it? I couldn't remember anyone closing the door. I tried the handle, and—with the lock broken—it easily turned in my hand.

"What are you doing?" Jonathan asked.

"The basement. That's where—"

"I know, where Homer Tavey fell down the stairs. Well, I don't want to waste time seeing the basement when we have better things to do."

I looked into Jonathan's eyes and asked, "Who pushed Mr. Tavey down the stairs? Who shoved the summer kitchen down on Mr. Merle? You or your grandmother?"

Jonathan took a sharp breath, and I could see the lie forming. "Yesterday evening Grandma and I were together at her house making popcorn and watching TV," he said, and laughed. "Solid alibis. Don't give it another thought."

"I won't," I assured him. "I'll let the sheriff

work it out. Since you're each other's alibi, with no other witnesses—"

"Nobody's gonna bother Grandma," Jonathan insisted. "She's a fixture in Bogue City, president of the Historical Society and all that. Sure, she'll do anything to get her own way, but other than that she's a nice, harmless, old lady. Right?"

Harmless? I didn't think so. I didn't think the sheriff would think she was so harmless, either, when I told him to check the windowsill and basement door for her fingerprints—Jonathan's, too. I was also counting on Jonathan's big mouth. Eventually, with his oversized ego, he'd want to brag, and he'd blab the whole story.

Jonathan took my hand from the doorknob and pulled me in his wake until we came to the parlor. "We don't want to stand around arguing, Lia. Let's make ourselves comfortable," he said.

As he flopped down on a sofa, yanking me down beside him, he slipped an arm around my shoulders, hugging me close. "This is nice," he murmured. "Too bad we didn't bring something to eat or a portable CD player."

I pushed against him and sat upright. "Sorry, Jonathan, but this isn't part of the plan."

"I've got plans, too," he said. He reached for me again, but I jumped to my feet.

A light breeze brushed my cheek, lifting tendrils of my hair. I was so scared, I wanted to run straight out of the house and never come back, but I couldn't. I took a deep breath and said, "Listen, Jonathan. Be quiet and listen."

"I don't hear anything," he said.

But I did.

"Come upstairs with me," I told him. Dusk was quickly dissolving into darkness, so I turned on my flashlight.

"That's more like it," Jonathan said. He turned on his flashlight and tried to catch up with me as I ran through the entry hall, up the stairs, and into Placide Blevins's bedroom. When we were inside the room I shut the door and faced Jonathan.

"It's stronger here," I said, "The whispers have come. Do you hear them? Do you feel them pulling and pushing us, wrapping around our heads and poking at our minds?"

Jonathan took a step backward, bumping into the closed door. He looked pale. "Don't do that, Lia!" he said.

I could hear it clearly now, the whispered word repeated over and over, tumbling against itself, beating against my ears. And I knew what the voice was saying: "Below, below, below."

"Look at the ceiling, Jonathan," I said. "Look at the tiny faces and their mean, hard eyes. You can see their sharp teeth and their split little serpent tongues."

He looked upward and let out a yelp of terror. "What are they doing? What are they saying?" he cried.

A cold wind rushed through the room, lifting the curtains at the blank-eyed windows, and wrapped itself around us.

"You're not going to frighten me out of the house," I called out to the invisible one. "I know who you are and how to send you away from Graymoss."

Jonathan's eyes rolled up in his head. He slumped against the door, and I thought he would faint.

I reached out and shook his shoulder. "Get a grip on yourself," I shouted at him over the wind and the voices. "Come down to the basement with me. I need your help."

I reached for the doorknob, but Jonathan was faster. He shoved me aside and raced into the hall. I could hear him clattering down the stairs and into the kitchen. As I walked carefully down the stairs, gripping the handrail, I heard Jonathan's car driving away.

I was all alone. It was better that way.

The wind pushed against me. The whispers turned to shouts, and invisible fingers pulled through my hair and along my face. I had trouble breathing, and my feet became heavy, as though I were walking through thick mud. *Leave this horrible place!* a voice in my head kept saying. *Get out of here! Run!*

But I couldn't. I had to finish the task I'd come for. I struggled into the kitchen, where I tugged and jerked at the closed basement door. The winds had caught it and wouldn't let go. "You can't stop me!" I shouted. "I'm going to win!"

The door suddenly flew open, knocking me off balance. Carefully I crawled down the stairs, clinging to the railing. The beam from my flashlight made a path through the darkness, and I followed it.

With the wind and voices howling around me, I struggled to the back of the basement. I laid my flashlight on a shelf so that its beam hit the brick

181

wall between the arches. Then I picked up the wooden mallet and the short iron bar with the point on one end. Placing the point against the mortar between a row of bricks, I began to pound.

As chips of mortar and bricks flew, I cried out, "Mr. Blevins, I got your message. You never did say that Slade had left. You only told Charlotte that Slade wouldn't harm her. Now I know how you kept him from doing that."

A brick wobbled and fell out. I attacked the ones above and next to it.

Over the roaring in my ears I shouted, "You thought you were protecting Charlotte. You didn't know you were imprisoning Slade's evil in Graymoss."

Suddenly something soft and furry brushed against my legs, and I leaped back with a scream, dropping my iron bar.

I looked down to see the large black cat staring up at me. "Oh, it's you," I said, but I was breathing hard, and it took me a few moments to recover.

The cat patted at the iron bar, then hunched over it, glaring at me with his gleaming, yellow eyes.

"Move," I said, and bent to pick up the bar, but the cat snarled and hissed.

Was this a real cat or was it a visible part of the evil in Graymoss? I didn't want to find out, so I quit trying to retrieve the iron bar and reached for the flat iron tool with a handle instead. I hammered with all my strength at the mortar. The cat yowled and vanished into the darkness.

As I worked I shouted, "Morgan Slade, Mr.

Blevins had to stop you from harming his grand-daughter. And I'm going to stop you from harming Graymoss. You are the evil that haunts the house, but your power is gone! You're leaving! Now!"

With a final slam against the bricks, a section about two feet wide broke off and fell through. I picked up my flashlight and swept its beam through the hidden room on the other side of the wall.

The small room was dank and cobwebby, but there before me was the fine wine cellar, with rows and rows of bottles covered in a thick layer of dust. On the floor was spread the remnants of a deteriorated canvas sack, its contents of silver plate and jewelry spilled onto the ground. And next to the sack, facedown, with a bashed-in skull, lay the partly clothed skeleton of a man.

I remembered what the woman in the French Quarter had told me. Hoping I had the words right, I cleared my throat, made my voice as stern and loud as I could, and said, "Go away, Morgan Slade. Go to whatever awaits you."

The cold winds abruptly stopped, and the whispers stilled. The house was suddenly so quiet that I staggered back against the shelves. "I did it!" I said aloud. "I really did it!"

But I remembered there hadn't been just one ghost. Softly I added, "You can go, too, Mr. Blevins. Your house is now in good hands."

Graymoss would be inhabited by our family and a bunch of kids who might be a little noisy at times and might be a real pain in the neck at other times, but who needed to be part of a family. I was pretty sure Placide Blevins would approve.

And he'd approve of what I'd done to save Graymoss.

So would Mom and Dad. I'd tell them everything, and Mom would try to make it all seem logical so that I wouldn't be traumatized by ghosts or messages or anything she couldn't explain. But she'd be happy—ecstatically happy—because clearing the house of evil spirits would mean Mom and Dad's dream could come true.

And Grandma, who'd been totally spooked by this house? She'd be proud of me, too.

I climbed out of the house through the kitchen window, shut it carefully, and sat on the steps of the front veranda. Pulling Grandma's cell phone from my pack, I dialed the Bogue City operator and asked to speak to the sheriff.

While I waited, I mentally hung the WOMEN WHO ARE EXCEPTIONALLY BRAVE banner over the front door. Bigger and brighter than before, the golden names glittered, and I grinned with delight as I looked at them. There, down at the bottom— along with all the rest—was written LIA MARIE STAR- LING.

"Sheriff Fuller speaking," the sheriff said into my ear.

"Hello, Sheriff Fuller," I answered. "This is Lia Starling. I'd like to report a murder."

# ABOUT THE AUTHOR

Joan Lowery Nixon has been called the grande dame of young adult mysteries and is the author of more than a hundred books for young readers, including *Murdered, My Sweet; Don't Scream; Spirit Seeker; Shadowmaker; Secret, Silent Screams; A Candidate for Murder; Whispers from the Dead;* and the middle-grade novel *Search for the Shadowman*. Joan Lowery Nixon was the 1997 president of the Mystery Writers of America and is the only four-time winner of the Edgar Allan Poe Best Young Adult Mystery Award. She received the award for *The Kidnapping of Christina Lattimore, The Séance, The Name of the Game Was Murder,* and *The Other Side of Dark,* which also won the California Young Reader Medal. Her historical fiction includes the award-winning series The Orphan Train Adventures.

Joan Lowery Nixon lives in Houston with her husband.